THE BLUE GUIDE TO INDIANA

THE BLUE GUIDE TO INDIANA

Michael Martone

FC2

Normal/Tallahassee

Published by FC2 with support provided by Florida State University, the Unit for Contemporary Literature of the Department of English at Illinois State University, the Program for Writers of the Department of English of the University of Illinois at Chicago, the Illinois Arts Council, and the Florida Arts Council of the Florida Division of Cultural Affairs

Address all inquiries to: Fiction Collective Two, Florida State University, c/o English Department, Tallahassee, FL 32306-1580

ISBN: Paper, 1-57366-095-7

Library of Congress Cataloging-in-Publication Data
Martone, Michael.
  The blue guide to Indiana / Michael Martone.-- 1st ed.
    p. cm.
  ISBN 1-57366-095-7
  1. Indiana--Humor. I. Title.
  PS3563.A7414 B58 2001
  818'.5407--dc21
                                2001001419

Cover Design: Todd Michael Bushman
Book Design: Tara Reeser

Produced and printed in the United States of America
Printed on recycled paper with soy ink

Illinois **ARTS** Council
AN AGENCY OF
THE STATE OF ILLINOIS

This program is partially supported by a grant from the Illinois Arts Council

For
Pooch and the three Marys,
Lobrillo, West, and Keeler,
storytellers and travelers all

and in memory of
William Pappas

"Tell them Bill Pappas sent you!"

ACKNOWLEDGMENTS

Sections of this book appeared in *McSweeney's, Notre Dame Review, Dancing Star, Meridian, Another Chicago Magazine, 3rd Bed, Ascent, Italian Americana, Epoch, Bombay Gin, Arts Indiana, The Baffler, Bridge,* and *CutBank.* Excerpts also appeared in the newspapers *Breeze* and *Nuvo.* I thank all of the editors for publishing parts of *The Blue Guide to Indiana.* I would especially like to thank Jim Poyser whose newspapers cover the whole Hoosier State. I would like to thank R.M. Berry, Brenda Mills, Cris Mazza, Tara Reeser, and everyone associated with FC2. I thank my fellow cartographers—Sandy Huss, Robin Behn, Bruce Smith, Wendy Rawlings and the rest of the surveying crew working below the bug line in Tuscaloosa. I thank my field agents on the ground—Susan Neville, Mike Wilkerson and Deb Galyan, Kathy Hall and Leighton Pierce, Melanie Rae Thon, Safiya Henderson-Holmes, and Michael Rosen. Paul Maliszewski and Gary Pike provided the theoretical underpinnings. Marian Young contributed the practical logistics. Sam and Nick colored the maps. And thanks to Theresa Pappas for sextant, compass, chronograph, and GPS.

OTHER BOOKS BY MICHAEL MARTONE

Gary on $5 a Day

Pensées: The Thoughts of Dan Quayle

The Mystical Hills East of Fort Wayne: The Literary Biography of Richard Bach

Everything You Always Wanted to Know about Gattling Guns

The Flatness and Other Landscapes

Let's Go: Terre Haute

Hoosier Depression Glass and Price Guide

Elkhart and the Surrounding Towns After Dark

The Rough Guide to French Lick

WARNING

It seems very likely that many times of opening for museums and sites given hopefully in the text, coupled with general remarks in the Practical Information section, will be found incorrect. At the time of writing not even official publications would be held responsible for accuracy. The "Standard Times" has been subject to constant alteration and exceptions, depending on whether the desire of the authorities to open longer hours or of the staffs for shorter hours and higher wages had the upper hand. This has already led to sharp rises in entry fees and unforeseen failures to open at all, a situation long familiar in Italy and Greece.

TABLE OF CONTENTS

A LETTER FROM THE LIEUTENANT GOVERNOR
OF THE STATE OF INDIANA

There is no argument that the State of Indiana is the Birth place of Vice Presidents. Seven Hoosiers have held the second highest office in the land. Thirteen more have run unsuccessfully for the office. Indiana is, after all, the only state in the union which holds primary elections expressly for the selection of Vice President. Hence, the first lesson gleaned by the careful reader of this guide is that Indiana endows those of "second" station with boundless respect and all requisite power. Thus, the constitution of the state recognizes the Lieutenant Governor, that would be me, as the ultimate executive in our government, with the Governor serving mainly as President of our Senate and as "Designated Father of the Bride" in our traditional wedding service.

But our governmental uniqueness does not end there. Let me draw your attention to The John Chancellor Memorial Pavilion in downtown Indianapolis, designed by the architect Michael Graves, from which, in every national election since 1958, powerful microwave transmissions emanate at precisely a nanosecond after the closing of Indiana polling places, uplinking the expected information to news dissemination organizations everywhere. Once in space, the signal rebounds off orbiting dedicated satellites, also designed by the architect Michael Graves, and received instantaneously in New York City, indicating a clear Republican victory in order for Indiana to be "called" for the Republican candidate immediately upon the commencement of that evening's National News.

The building also contains a Baptistry where those public officials elected as Democrats gather during their ritual conversion to Republican status. Now this realignment of party affiliation is standard for every politician in this state (I myself have run and won various offices as a Democrat three times, each time renouncing the party and becoming a Republican upon election). The Baptistry hosts many out-of-state conversions as well. Delightful quirks such as the above, unique to our state, hint at the many other distinctive features of Indiana chronicled by this guide.

The state, recognizing the value of your visit, now offers the only Ph.D. in tourism in the country at its Bloomington campus of Indiana University where out-of-state tuition is less than that paid by those in-state. The degree can easily be obtained during your two-week jaunt through the state if you utilize the regional campuses and distant learning facilities. Revenue from the tourism industry, according to the 1990 census, contributes nearly two-thirds of our state's gross income (coming in ahead of agriculture and hard currency derived from out-of-state relatives sending checks and money orders to their locally domesticated kin).

It is my honor also to introduce you to our newly renovated rest areas located a few feet inside every border. Here political appointees gladly greet you, the visitor, with refreshing pawpaw canapes and free glasses of buttermilk cider drawn from our state's native bison herds.

Those of you relocating to Indiana will find this edition of this guide indispensable to your relocation. Though I was born above my father's hobby store in Atwood, I myself found the following information informative. From the seismic hills outside Etna to the deepest coal mines down around Evansville, you will find this guide a godsend for your orientation to your new home. This book will help you find all of it. Bring your cameras to record each corner of the state's picturesque beauty from the excitement of our sporting events to the annual draining of the swamps, from the blessing of the crop-dusting fleet to the continual sweeping of the front porch steps by the widows of North Judson.

Be sure to visit me in my office at the State House, and I'll be happy to show you the famous desk (its top cut in the shape of Indiana and made from weathered planks taken from the teakwood deck of the USS Indiana). I will gladly present you with a complimentary bottle washer, manufactured by our sister state of Xi Juan, in the People's Republic of China, and a vial of rancid though medicinal French Lick's Own World Famous Pluto Springs Water, the secret ingredient of this, the most regular state in the union. Indiana!

Indianapolis
2001

PRACTICAL INFORMATION

What to Wear

Indiana's ambient temperature
is a mild mean of 54 degrees
Fahrenheit. The state is considered in the temperate zone, and
its climate supports a deciduous
woodland ecology, though

much of the native forest and swamp was eliminated in the
19th century or has retreated underground to form clandestine niches in the area's many caves and caverns. The
visitor should pack for rain and snow as the state experi-
ences "lake effect" precipitation, located as it is on the leeside
of Lake Michigan and in the Great Lakes basin. Snowfall
can be expected, for this reason, as late as June. Mosquito
netting and light clothing are also recommended, as Indiana is home to 837 sub-species of the insect, aggressively
incubated in the state's few remaining bogs and marshes,
as well as in the state mosquito hatcheries. The concentration of the mosquito infestation makes the population ex-
tremely competitive and host to a wide variety of interesting and colorful parasites for which the mosquitoes serve
as vectors. Native dress, which is still worn routinely by
the local population, includes the baseball cap, Indian
beaded belt, and argyle rayon hose. Poplin windbreaker
and fingerless woolen gloves for males, and halter tops,
plastic barrettes, and acid-washed denim jeans for females
are common attire. Tribal affiliations are often subtle and
involve bandana kerchiefs worn in ritual knotted styles, and
colorful canvas and rubber basketball footwear. Visitors

are asked to refrain from including such clothing in their
travel wardrobe as it is often simple to give offense, and
the consequences of such misunderstanding are many times
severe and dramatic.

Currency

Indiana recognizes the legal tender of
the United States of America but today
also circulates other currency within its
borders. S&H Green Stamps issued mid-
century are particularly popular, as are
coupons gleaned from Bel Air cigarettes when bundled in
rubber band bound packs of 500. Descendants of immi-
grant Venetians who operate a barter-based culture in the
lake and canal district of northern Indiana have issued a
scrip from time to time which you are invited to counterfeit when and wherever possible. The selling of futures has
become quite popular, due perhaps to the proximity of the
Chicago Mercantile Exchanges. A significant percentage
of the population engages in the trading of weather futures,
the result of which is the amassing of one of the largest
fortunes in the country controlled by the Sanders brothers
of Nashville, who also have a major stake in the franchise
on the coloring used in hardwood tree foliage each fall.
There is also a lively business to be made in scrap copper
wire which is utilized by the state's vast magnet wire and
cable cartel. During periods of copper panic, the electrical
systems of inhabited houses have been known to be stolen
outright while their owners sleep. Routine business is often performed using pennies, exclusively, whose value fluc-
tuates daily, the price being fixed at 8:30 each morning at
the Copper Exchange in New Haven. A tradition is to
present young girls with spools of thread gauge copper
wire on their namedays (see page 25). The thread is used
later in the sewing of their wedding trousseaus.

Getting There

Indiana may be reached by packet boat
and rail handcar operated as a concession by the remnants of the Miami tribal
council. There are a variety of commuter

flights scheduled to arrive daily at the
various international airports, the appellation "international" denoting the fact that the air traveler needs to pass
through Canadian or Mexican airports to connect with
those flights. The last railroad car float runs between
Windsor, Ontario, and Fort Wayne. The motorist will note
that the highway gauge switches from the standard dimen-
sion to the narrow one upon entering the state and that
one's tires must be changed out at the border to accommo-
date the change. Many travelers arrive in the state by means
of tramp van line. Cruising freight trucks plying transcon-
tinental routes provide a few berths to the traveler not
pressed for time. Amenities, while not always to the standard of luxury found on the bus lines, are often quite comfortable and include staterooms, buffets, swimming pools,
and a traveling driving range atop the trailer.

The Time

Indiana does not participate in Daylight Savings Time and is, ostensively,
on Eastern Standard Time the year
round. However, time has always been
problematic here (two civil wars have
been fought over the time), and the

traveler should not depend on any modern systematic reck-
oning of the hour while in the state. Most municipalities,
townships, and county governments maintain an Office of
Time and an elected Keeper who shoots sun time daily,
fixing the noon zenith as an official and local reference.
Some kind of broadcast device (in most cases a tornado
siren or air-raid klaxon) then issues a local alarm in order

for residents to set their own clocks and watches. This is somewhat complicated each spring during the tornado season and was quite disruptive during the early days of the Second World War. This issue is further exacerbated in the southern counties (in which President Lincoln lived as a boy) where the clocks must, by law, always read ten till ten, the moment of Lincoln's assassination. Consequently, the citizenry there maintains, simultaneously, a secret set of clocks which always measures time relative to 9:50. This may cause such circumlocutions as, "The time is three hours and forty-seven minutes before ten till ten."

Tipping

Indiana rickshaw drivers routinely expect seven and a half percent of the metered fare and one dollar for each bag handled. Standard practices of tipping apply to those who serve food, though they will also accept strands of wire, and in the case of cocktail bar and tavern employees it is not necessary to strip the colored plastic insulating the wire and is usually considered an insult or an indication of the customer's dissatisfaction if stripped wire is left as a tip. There is one doorman in the state, and his services are provided gratis to the public, as he is supported by endowment from the state's canal royalties. He does however expect a Christmas present each year, and his current hat, collar, and waist size are posted on the day after Thanksgiving at the corner of Washington and Meridian in a third floor window of the old L.S. Ayres building in Indianapolis.

Phones, Mail, Telegraph

Indiana supports a network of freestanding kiosks maintained by the blind. Usually painted red and located in parking lots adjacent to shopping centers, the kiosks are open 24 hours a day. In addition to dispensing confections and reading material, these kiosks provide, for a surcharge, access to the telephonic, telegraphic, and postal systems of communication. Indiana is the last state to provide self-service telegraph keys to the consumer. The kiosks are also the source for important travel information, maps, snake-bite kits, spiral mosquito coil repellant, postcards, shoe-strings, currency exchange, and film for the camera. The kiosks serve as the de facto birth control clinics for the state, providing a variety of products to those 14 years and older.

Inoculations and Required Vaccines

Indiana has one living American Elm tree. It is preserved in a specially constructed arboretum on Elm Street in Elmsville. Consequently, the state requires visitors to provide documentation attesting to inoculation against the Dutch Elm Disease. The state parasite is ringworm, which is, as ringworm is a fungus, also the state fungus. Thus ringworm is a protected species as is its habitat. As of August 1955, the state has suffered an outbreak of hepatitis H which requires the wearing of plastic gloves by everyone at all times *except* when eating. Allergies to latex and PVC gloves are pandemic. Most municipal water supplies have been treated with fluoride as have all sources of Eucharist bread and wafers. The vaccine to ward off crying is suggested for those planning to visit Indiana, as are boosters to prevent dreaming and whistling.

Where to Stay

Indiana has an extensive state-adminis-
tered motel chain considered "B" class
lodging. Reservations can be made at any
kiosk for any room in the state. The bright
blue Quonset Huts of the state motels are
often found near bus terminals and the
many bucolic basketball parks. Camping is frowned upon,
as it is not understood by the typical Hoosier, though private and public yurt grounds are available throughout the
state. Many private homes offer lodging, and it is not inap-
propriate to ask to see the room, usually in the basement,
before settling on a price. Rooms are also brokered through
an 800 number. Complete hotels or single family cabins
can be constructed overnight on any public commons by
roving manufacturing crews representing the mobile and
modular home interests near Nappanee. First Class accommodations are scarce but are represented by the resorts at
French Lick and West Baden Springs, now mainly used by
retired mobsters from Chicago who still have their private
railcars parked on sidings on the resorts' grounds. Don't
overlook the former tuberculosis sanatoriums and state
hospitals for the insane, their patients now mainstreamed
into the general population. The physical plants of these
institutions have been refitted to provide Deluxe accommodations in a Victorian setting. Indiana is considered by
the hospitality industry to suffer a surplus of medium-priced
rooms, so reservations are rarely required. Only in the winter months should the traveler take the precaution of calling ahead. During that season, accommodations are sometimes taxed, as African and Indonesian anthropology ma-
jors are most likely to be "walking in" to the towns and
villages of their subject population.

Transportation

Indiana is the home of the last vestige
of the once extensive interurban light
rail network, a creature of the electrical
production and transmission companies
that provided the power for the high
speed trolleys and the rights of way be-
neath their wires for track. The Chicago, South Shore, and
South Bend (C,SS&SB) still operates daily in a commuter
capacity between those namesake cities.

Traffic safety has always been a major concern for the citizens of the state. The first fatality in the nation associated
with a traffic light occurred in Fort Wayne when the eight
year old Maurice Norton, crossing with the light at Jefferson
and Calhoun, was run down by a Maxwell Demon piloted
by a driver from Ohio. Today, everyone who drives in the
state must qualify to do so. In addition to the standard
motor vehicle testing, drivers must also earn a special cer-
tificate awarded after extensive training at the Grant County
Safety Village outside Marion. This half-size replication of
streetscapes, super highways, and country market roads
simulates a variety of real life driving hazards and responses.
Yearly, on the anniversary of the mishap, the safety village
stages the historical pageant commemorating the automotive accident which took the life of native son, James Dean,
whose performing double, drawn from Fairmount Junior
High School's 8th grade, is selected through a rigorous
competitive process. The accident is lovingly staged and
produced by the school's chapter of the Future Farmers of
America and 4-H.

Indiana supports competing statewide chains of jin rickshaw fleets, the Safety and the Checker companies. By law,
rickshaws for hire must be painted yellow and be equipped
with a meter to distinguish them from the privately operated rickshaws. These rickshaws for hire operate locally
but can be retained for intrastate travel along the converted

interurban rail right of ways between larger metropolitan areas.

If using the federal interstate highway system in the region, be aware that I-72 is an "air-line" whose roadway transverses the entire state, elevated on concrete pylons from Terra Haute to Richmond, having no exits or entrances to Indiana below this limited access corridor. Rest areas and service stations are provided at suspended platforms spaced evenly along the route.

Indiana, due to its favorable laws concerning interstate commerce, is home to several major moving and transfer companies. During summer months the cities of Evansville, Indianapolis, and Fort Wayne (homes of the larger companies based here) often experience crippling gridlock as the fleets of vans congregate in these headquarter cities to shift loads, re-route deliveries, and dispatch expedited merchandise. Fort Wayne, home of North American Van Lines, for example, sees a concentration of nearly a quarter million trucks during the summer migration, about one van per resident. It is not rare to witness many complete living room ensembles or bedroom suites assembled on lawns, in parks, or upon parking lots as the contents of the moves are redistributed using any available space for the sorting. Indiana has become, therefore, a haven for the amateur truck watcher during this season, and many travel from Europe or Asia to record these new sightings, perhaps to register that rare Peterbilt or International cabover.

As one might gather of the state where the automobile was invented, walking is frowned upon. Shoes and shoe leather are heavily taxed, and shoe repair is a clandestine and shady black market enterprise. In addition to stamping license plates, the state's inmate population also provides electrical power through the co-production of current generated by punitive treadmill sentences at the state penitentiary in Michigan City. Those who walk are often detained by police using profiling procedures which target pedestrians as likely carriers of controlled substances.

Birthdays and Namedays

Birthdays are not celebrated in Indiana, but namedays are. The calendar of these days can be found in any phone book and the appropriate card available at the neighborhood kiosk. The celebration usually consists of visiting everyone one knows so named on the particular day set aside to celebrate those so named. The traditional gift is often a calendar of namedays and/or the new edition of the phone book

SOME MAJOR CITIES AND TOWNS

Fort Wayne

Here, an exact replica of the original, early nineteenth-century American fort stands right downtown (tours available). Authentically dressed interpreters recreate a summer's day in 1816 through a thoroughly detailed living history re-enactment. Visitors often attempt to trick the fort's employees into revealing their actual twenty-first-century predilections. More fascinating is the elaborate modern wall which protects the fort (tours available). Constructed of cyclone fencing, galvanized corrugated steel sheets, and locally fabricated concertina wire, this outer wall contrasts strikingly with the wooden walls it guards. The modern Fort Wayne is itself enclosed by a connected system of breastworks and ramparts, copies of famous European fortifications and castles. A walking tour of its parapeted walls makes for a great day outing. Under construction in the suburbs, yet another wall of imported timber and carbon polymer resins nears completion along the city's busy beltway. Beyond that, excavation is under way for an encircling moat in whose waters the remaining fields of corn will be reflected. And in a north-side park, a small museum (free) provides a history of defenses. Scale models of star forts' geometric ravelins, bastions, glacis, and covered ways are encased in clear glass cases.

Gas City

Here, in the last century, extensive deposits of iodine ore were discovered near an unnamed, sleepy crossroads village. The discovery started the Tincture Boom of 1869 and led to the naming of the resulting metropolis of wooden shacks and Civil War surplus canvas tents as Gas City. The name was inspired by the many violet plumes of pure iodine gas which continually hung over the town. The gas, a by-product of the smelting process which utilizes the sub-lime property of iodine to metamorphose from a solid to a gas when heated, was often so thick as to force the lighting of the halogen lamps at noon. The resulting purple atmosphere was said to have medicinal properties. Toward the turn of the last century, its iodine mines played out, the city enjoyed a brief revival as a spa, catering to visiting wealthy elites who would take the airs. The grand hotels of this era and the palatial mansions of the iodine barons, many now renovated as bed-and-breakfasts, line Antiseptic Avenue. Each summer, using the traditional methods, Gas Citizens still cut dry ice from the Dioxide River, loading the steaming blocks in box cars for shipment to ice cream vendors of major cities.

McNally Junction

Here, the visitors center (First and A streets) traces this town's unique history. To protect the information copyrighted on their maps, mapmakers often label imaginary places in their renderings. Thus, a quick review of a competitor's charts will reveal whether the whole design has been copied wholesale when the bogus town appears there as if real. Located on the site where a "McNally Junction" was supposed to be, McNally Junction was hastily settled by a colony of cartographers after their company was sued by a rival firm which planted the trap. Nearby (Second and B Streets), a plaque commemorates the judge's on-site inspection to ascertain the veracity of the claims. By then, the cartographers had hurriedly constructed a clutch of houses, five identical shells each newly painted one of the five colors used to tint countries. The smell of paint drying is, therefore, important to the residents who grow, in their formal map-colored gardens, flowers which produce, when dried, an odious potpourri mixture capturing that heady scent. A gift shop is located in The Sienna House (Third and C Streets) where one can also buy a variety of maps of this, now, the most mapped spot on earth.

New Harmony

Here, the streets of this lovely village are lined with ginkgo trees (*Ginkgo biloba*). Native to China, the trees, the oldest deciduous species in the world, were planted in the hundreds by the Harmonites, the first of two utopian settlements to occupy the town. The Harmonites believed in a multiplicity of times, spending theirs in the precise measure of diurnal, lunar, tidal, seasonal, gestational cycles and their intersections with this place they called New Harmony. Notice the many ruins of their famous moondials and inspect, in the museum (slight charge), the many menstruations logbooks. Today's town bustles with modern unreligious inhabitants routinely setting their wristwatches via a phone call to a recording, ignoring the seemingly irregular blasts emanating from the ancient automated Harmonite steam whistles. Every autumn, the town celebrates its festival. Busloads of tourists, some coming from as far away as China, gather to witness the spontaneous falling of the ginkgo foliage. This phenomenon, still unexplained, cannot be predicted accurately. One can only estimate the narrow band of time when the slant of the sun, the temperature, and the duration of starlight signals in the prehistoric trees the simultaneous and complete release of every fan-like leaf.

Rising Sun

Here, as elsewhere in this region, the inhabitants of Rising Sun have placed their factories on the village's eastern boundary, all the better to allow the effluent of their industry to flow downstream, so to speak, in the prevailing wind. However, here the natives serve an immediate market by manufacturing, each morning, the day itself and construct the special apparatus necessary to levitate the daily details of light and color above the town. The nation's third largest consumer of helium, Rising Sun is famous for its fleet of cloud-camouflaged blimps and squadrons of transparent zeppelins which lift the dyed gel flats of sky into the sky. Wingwalkers on jump-jets spot-weld each afternoon's I-beamed dome of heaven; gyrocopters tow V-strings of simulated waterfowl in migration; helicopters hover, hanging the bright first-order Fresnel lens which counterfeits the evening star. Not to be missed are the quaint cyanine works (tours daily) where the invention of a new blue is routine. The craftsmen of Rising Sun build into their work an obsolescence. Each night the remnants of the day can be seen drifting overhead as odd-shaped shadows shift beneath what is thought to be a real, though often disappointing, moon.

South Bend

Here, the classic movie, *The Philadelphia Story*, plays daily each midnight at the restored St. Joe Theater downtown. The picture has been shown this way continuously since shortly after its premiere in 1940. These performances are events, with the audience members dressing as their favorite characters played on film by Katherine Hepburn, Cary Grant, James Stewart and many others. Having memorized the dialogue, the movie's fans also act out the more memorable scenes, speaking directly to and along with the actors on the screen. Fans break golf clubs and re-enact the punch in the snout, the meeting in the library, and even blow the trumpet for the fox hunt. The recitation of the script, while choral, is quite exact and perfectly inflected. Many participants bring their own models of the yacht, *True Love*, and repeat in unison that she is "yar" as if cheering at a football game. Without a doubt, the most impressive and mesmerizing ritual surrounds the exchange between Miss Hepburn and Mr. Stewart concerning the nativity of Mr. Stewart's character. He reports that he is from South Bend, which elicits from the audience thunderous applause. But Miss Hepburn's response inevitably sends the house into ecstasy. "South Bend," she says. "It sounds like dancing." Whereupon the whole evening's audience begins to waltz throughout the building on the stage and in the balconies, the lobbies and stairwells, often spilling back out to Colfax Avenue, stopping what little traffic there is at that time of night.

Bristol

Here, in 1875, Albert Einstein, while filming another instructional movie explaining his theory of general relativity (this time using the Doppler effects of the New York Central's crack streamliner, The Twentieth Century Limited, as it tore across the state to illustrate the concept), visited a local tourist curiosity called "The Blue Hole" where an enterprising local charged two bits to observe an azure opening in the air. There, Professor Einstein realized that this "Blue Hole" was simply another anticipated rip in the fabric of time and space. The savvy reader will have realized as well, at this point, that the Professor, in 1875, had yet to be born (nor had the motion picture and the train, named for a century that hadn't happened yet, been invented). The actual filming took place in a barely existing 1939. Now, today, whenever you read this, it is the site of a factory manufacturing aspirin for exportation. The disruption in the continuum continues and contributes to the phenomenon, reported by many, of residents being stricken by a series of excruciating headaches and migraines and other debilitating cerebral electrical disruptions. These include perceptual disorientations of all the senses and of all kinds, including, especially, the phenomena of serial deja vu whose deja vu-ed images of this place's particular history often overwhelm the victim, rendering him or her spastic and disoriented. A visitor quickly senses an uncanny pattern of sameness to the days here and reports sensations of dread and despair surrounding the phrase, "The Good Old Days," and upon innocently entering the cafe on the town square.

THE DEATH TOUR

Site of Wendell Willkie's Ascension into Heaven
Seven Miles South and West of Rushville
Homer

Outside Rushville, a modest plaque and an eternal "flame" mark the site of Wendell Willkie's bodily assumption into the heavens over Indiana on a summer's day in 1944. Willkie, originally a Democrat, ran as the Republican candidate for president in 1940 only to lose to Franklin D. Roosevelt who was elected for an unprecedented third term. Willkie was an unlikely candidate for the nation's highest elective office. Not a professional politician or war hero, Willkie was the executive of an electric power company who championed the expansion of the interurban rail network and fought the imposition of the Tennessee Valley Authority. His presidential campaign is today remembered by historians mainly for the first extensive use of the celluloid button imprinted with a variety of clever slogans worn by his supporters to advertise his candidacy. The saying, "What'd you want, a Willkie button?" derives from this widespread practice. Near the site, high-tension transmission towers converge on the sacred precinct of an Indiana Power and Light substation where mighty step-down transformers convert the mega-voltage to power the single 75-watt flame-shaped bulb of the eternal votive light. The Republican Party maintains a perpetual sentry post here where tradition demands that visitors, through their crazy antics, attempt to elicit a smile from the always sober, flannel-suited guardsman.

Sunset Lawns and the Bronze Mortuary
The Cemetery at Naked City
Roselawn

Outside the walls of the nation's largest and most popular nudist colony, enclosed within its own ten foot palisade of ivy-covered, sun-cured California redwood, is the Cemetery at Naked City. Landscaped by Frederick Law Olmstead, the designer of New York's Central Park, the seventy-five acres of rolling wooded hills serve as a final resting place for hundreds of this nation's most enthusiastic sun-enthusiasts all of whom have been interred here in the nude. Designed to offer a contemplative sanctuary for the visitor and family-member alike, the cemetery provides detailed maps to the plots of the more notable permanent residents while encouraging the non-grieving bird-watcher and mushroom hunter as well. Clothing is optional as you stroll through the groves of quaking Lombardy poplars, reading the telling epitaphs on the impressive undressed marble headstones. The Bronze Mortuary, on the grounds, provides funeral parlors, chapels, and changing rooms for those attending the final rites of the recently departed. At the wakes, only the simplest of net veils are suggested for the ladies. The tanned remains of the recently departed are viewed, in their all-together, reposing, peacefully, on clear plastic air mattresses in specially designed polished and transparent Plexiglass coffins.

The Grave of Anton "Spink" Payne
Payne Holler
Crown Hill Cemetery
Indianapolis

Outside of the occasional visits by some of the deer which inhabit the 500-acre grounds of the cemetery, no one now visits the grave of Anton "Spink" Payne, the inventor of the field tiling system which bears his name, and engineer responsible for the successful agricultural drainage of

Indiana's Limberlost Swamp. Where the Hoosier poet laureate, James Whitcomb Riley, rests at the crown of Crown Hill's Strawberry Peak, Marion County's highest point, Spink Payne is buried a few hundred yards away at its lowest spot, Payne Holler, whose sinkhole opens into the northernmost reaches of southern Indiana's limestone karst region of extensive subterranean caverns and underground rivers. A contemporary of Riley's and immortalized by him in verse, Spink was a beloved character throughout the state, traveling its length and breadth via the honeycomb network of sewers, sluiceways, aqueducts, and caves to emerge unexpectedly in, say, the filtration plant of Hobart or a cesspool of Versailles. School children loved him and grade school classes routinely visited him at his home, a ruined lock house near Delphi on the Wabash Canal. Eulogizing him at his funeral, Riley addressed a crowd numbering in the thousands, and referred to Spink as a man "whose heaven was the bowels of Indiana, happy, now, and at home at last!"

The Federal Research and Testing Center
for Coffin and Casket Standards
Tony Hulman Industrial Park
Batesville

Outside this sprawling, state of the-art facility, dozens of simulated gravesites are personally monitored by crack teams of research scientists from the vantage of underground booths adjacent to the decaying burial apparati and visually accessible by means of unique glass-walled cutaway crypts. During month-long shifts at their subterranean stations, the researchers record their findings using such indexes as accumulated hydrodynamics, putrefaction, and the proliferation of nematode and maggot infestations, while filming the process in the miracle of time-lapsed photography. Above ground, other technicians perform exhaustive testing on every make and model of casket and coffin marketed in America's graveyards and cemeteries. Special machines repeatedly slam lids. Silk linings and pillows are set on fire. Caskets are dropped from bone-jarring heights. Seals and gaskets endure the high pressures generated in the massive wind tunnels. Most interesting is the preparation of the test "corpses" for burial. Obsolete crash test dummies, designated as surplus by the National Highway Safety Council, are then "dressed" by experts in an organic "flesh" of a meat-like substance invented by the center's own staff before being placed on-board the test platform and lowered into the very real earth.

The Tomb of Orville Redenbacher
Valparaiso

Outside the tomb proper, one approaches through a maze of demonstration plots displaying plantings of varietal popcorn strains developed by Orville Redenbacher when he was an agricultural extension agent. During the growing season, hand-picked Hoosier high-schoolers perform the necessary tasks of detasseling and deroguing the plants and enthusiastically discuss with the visitor the intriguing sex life of corn. The tomb of corrugated steel sheeting and weathered barnwood, designed by the architect Michael Graves, is an exact reproduction of the Indiana pavilion constructed for the Chicago's Columbian Exhibition of 1894, which itself reproduces the exact dimensions of the Parthenon on the Acropolis in Athens. The marble of the Doric-order columns has been replaced with glass, encasing, within the pillar, a colorful array of unpopped kernels of corn. The frieze reproduces the history of maize in America and its transmission to a grateful Europe. Bring binoculars to view the fifty-six metopes which are carved to narrate the life of Orville Redenbacher. The third panel shows the infant Orville nursing at the breast of Demeter and Ceres. The twenty-fourth details the procedure for tying a bow tie. The thirty-ninth commemorates the invention of the microwave. Each spring, the citizens of Valparaiso and Porter County re-enact the grand procession from the

tomb to the birthplace, in a Lutheran version of the ancient Eleusinian Mysteries.

The National Monument for Those Killed by Tornados in Trailer Parks and Mobile Home Courts
Intersection of US 33 and Indiana 119
Goshen

Outside the memorial cenotaph is the famous cinder block
wall where the names of those who lost their lives during
cyclonic conditions are inscribed by Amish craftsmen with
ten-penny nails. Mementos left here by visitors are collected
and displayed in the adjacent museum—half of a double-
wide mobile home where such personal effects may be
viewed through the 100-mil plastic sheeting which covers
the open wall. The cenotaph itself is carved from Bedford
limestone by Italian emigrants who have worked on European cathedrals and is sculpted to resemble a life-sized reproduction of an Airstream trailer. Surrounded by an intensive complex of working factories dedicated to the manufacturing of recreational vehicles, van conversions, fifth
wheels, trailers, mobile homes, and cyclone fencing, the
memorial is bathed in the ambient noise of whirlwind construction. This cacophony is only interrupted by the rigor-
ously scheduled, specially chartered freight train which
roars back and forth on the siding track hard-by the site,
triggering the warning blasts of antique sirens and creating
a sound, it is said by the old-timers who serve as guides,
just like that of a real tornado.

THE CUISINE

The Trans-Indiana Mayonnaise Pipeline
from Aurora in the east to East Chicago in the west
Visitors Center at Bennett's Switch,
Intersection of US 31 and Indiana 18

Conceived and built during the first Eisenhower administration, the Trans-Indiana Mayonnaise Pipeline is the long-
est mayonnaise pipeline in the world. Designed to transport the viscous condiment from the oil-rich soybean fields
and efficient egg ranches of east central and north central
Indiana to the bottling works of Kraft in Chicago, and Proctor and Gamble in Cincinnati, the Trans-Indiana pumps
3,000 barrels of sandwich spread a day through a system
of five-inch gauge refrigerated PVC tubing suspended above
the lush green fields of legumes and free-range chicken
ranches. Pumping substations, spaced conveniently every
ten miles along the route, provide the overlapping protection of massive condensing freon units and produce the
sustained 89-pound per square inch pressure along the line.
These stations also allow for local access to transmission
by the myriad of Hoosier mom and pop mayonnaise entre-
preneurs who add their product to the stream. The massive extent of this public work elicited extensive public
debate in the fifties, pitting local conservation and trucking
interests against the compelling national need for a readily
available, abundant, and inexpensive public source of salad
and sandwich dressing. This confrontation has been credited with sparking the environmental movement in Indiana. The construction of the pipeline, it was argued, would
disrupt the breeding grounds of the Greensburg Bison herd

and disrupt its seasonal migration range between Muncie and Milan. In response to such concerns, the pipeline follows an almost parallel course with Indiana's eastern border until it reaches Bethel above Richmond where it turns west into the interior. The pipeline also has, as part of its design, a series of buffalo ladders to facilitate the unencumbered migration of the Greensburg herd. One may glimpse portions of the pipeline best when the line intersects the north/south running turnpikes. When this occurs, the pipeline extends over the right-of-way in impressive sweeping white arches, since underground construction would tempt freezing during the severe and sustained winters. The Visitors Center at Bennett's Switch has several dioramic displays of the line's construction, a working slurry valve and vacuum pump, a scale model of the pipeline used by the Army Corps of Engineers to simulate various contingencies affecting the project and its product flow, a documentary on the life cycle of the Greensburg Bison with several preserved specimens, and a period concession stand where the bologna sandwiches are dressed by mayonnaise fresh from the nearby continually throbbing pipeline.

Annual Baking Powder Festival
Commemorating the Great Explosion of 1879
The Landing
Fort Wayne

Indiana is known as the Baking Powder Capital of the World. Many contemporary brands (including Rumford and Calumet) of the magical quick-acting leavening agent are still manufactured in or around Terre Haute, the result of an interesting historical confluence of events surrounding the controversy arising from the use of other ingredients in the mixture besides phosphate (see the entry on The Wars of Alum Succession). Less well-known is that baking powder was invented in Fort Wayne in 1866 by the druggists Joseph and Cornelius Hoagland and Thomas Biddle in the backroom of their shop located at the corner of Calhoun and The Landing of the Erie and Wabash Canal and where, in various conditions, they continued to manufacture the product as Royal Baking Powder until 1905. According to Griswold's *Pictorial History of Fort Wayne*, "Joseph Hoagland declined an offer of $12 million for his holdings" in 1893. The current Old Drug Building at 526 Calhoun Street (on the National Register of Historic Places) replaced the original building devastated in a catastrophic 1879 explosion of the volatile chemicals used to produce the powder. The initial conflagration and the subsequent firestorm it sparked consumed five city blocks, destroyed the adjoining Nickel Plate Railroad yard and station, and unearthed the old canal which had been filled in fifteen years before. In commemoration of this event and in celebration of the original creation of the indispensable household product, the proud citizens of Fort Wayne hold a festival each spring featuring the largest cake walk in the world (according to several sources) and a gigantic outdoor pageant in which hundreds of grade-school children enact the allegoric overthrow of European Yeast by the miracle of American pharmacological and nutritional science.

Recipes from <u>Cooking Plain</u>
by Helen Walker Linsenmeyer

Here is a selection of our favorite Midwestern recipes which suggest the diverse range of basic ingredients and satisfy nutritional requirements. The inventiveness of their preparation and presentation is also obvious. The following "taste" of Hoosier cuisine represents a few of the beloved preparations passed from generation to generation.

Pork Cake

Indiana's other white meat here becomes the baker's secret ingredient. Salt pork steps in for other rich shortenings in this tasty treat, demonstrating, at the same time, the spontaneous improvisational spirit of Hoosier homemakers caught short on staples.

1 pound salt pork
2 cups boiling water
1 pound raisins, coarsely chopped
1/4 pound citron, shaved fine
1 pound dates (optional)
2 cups dark brown sugar
1 cup molasses
1 teaspoon baking soda
4 cups white flour (more if necessary)
teaspoon each cinnamon, ground clove, allspice, nutmeg, salt

Chop pork very fine or put through grinder using medium blade. Pour boiling water over it. Add raisins, citron, dates, and brown sugar, stirring well to soften fruit. Stir soda into molasses and blend with pork. Sift flour with spices and salt and beat into liquid mixture, adding more flour if needed for stiff batter. Turn into a large loaf pan or bundt ring which has been well-greased and floured. Bake at 350 for an hour or more. Test for doneness by inserting a toothpick in the center of cake. If it comes out clean, cake is done. This cake will keep well if wrapped in foil or placed in tin container or dipped in liquid paraffin and allowed to harden. Powdered sugar may be dusted lightly over the top if desired.

Marshmallows

The marshmallow, long identified as the coup de grace on many a Hoosier dessert, is now often employed as a colorful side dish in and of itself and has made its appearance beside croutons, bacon bits, and potato sticks on the many famous Indiana Salad Bars. (See the entry on The Thirty Years Salad Bar War.)

1 ounce gum arabic
3 1/2 ounces confectioners' extra fine sugar
1/2 teaspoon vanilla
cornstarch

Cover gum arabic (can be obtained from your pharmacy) with 4 tablespoons of water and let stand for an hour. Heat in a double boiler until dissolved. Strain through cheesecloth and whip in the sugar. Set over fairly low fire and beat constantly for 45 minutes until mixture fluffs to stiff white froth. Remove from fire and beat 2 or 3 minutes while cooling, stirring in vanilla. Sift cornstarch into 8-by-8 inch pan to cover bottom, pour in the marshmallow mixture, smooth surface with back of spoon, and sift corn starch lightly over the top. When cold, cut into squares with sharp knife dipped in cornstarch, roll squares in the starch, and pack in tin which can be tightly covered.

Cottage Cheese

This exotic and creamy fromage, considered by most Indianans a downstate delicacy and specialty, is often made even more compelling by the addition of pinches of chopped chives or chopped parsley or by stirring in heaping spoonfuls of tangy tomato catsup.

1 gallon sour unpasteurized milk
1 teaspoon salt

1 tablespoon butter
sweet milk, about 2 tablespoons

Set a pan of sour, unpasteurized milk on stove over a very
low flame or over the pilot light and allow to remain until
the whey rises to the top. Do not let boil as this will cause
cheese to become hard and tough. Pour into cloth bag and
let it drain for two or three hours. Remove from bag and
chop fine with spoon. Add salt and butter and sufficient
sweet milk to soften. Refrigerate or set in cool place.

Snow Ice Cream
Made famous by the continental chefs of the Resort at West
Baden Springs where the dessert, it is said, was concocted
for either Al Capone or President Harding, snow ice cream
has become a standard confection at many of the state's
four-star hotels and ballroom venues including the Indiana Roof in Indianapolis, the Hotel Roberts in Muncie,
the Toboggan Run at Pokagon State Park, and Chez Michel
Jackson in Gary.

1 heaping china bowl of freshly fallen snow
maple syrup or warmed honey
some more snow

Fill china bowl with snow, pour syrup or honey over it,
and set bowl outside again nested in more snow. Wait
awhile. Serve with chilled silver spoon and eat immediately.

The Annual Eyeless Fish Fry
Marengo

Sponsored each fall by the Marengo Volunteer Fire Department, the annual Eyeless Fish Fry has become a staple of the southern Indiana foliage season. Marengo, located next to the Hoosier National Forest and upon the geological limestone karst plain of disappearing rivers and massive underground caverns, attracts thousands each year for the scenery and the fine eating. The many caves of the region provide perfect habitat for the local species of eyeless catfish that have, in their totally lightless environment, evolved without any need of light-sensing apparatus. The darkness in which they spawn has also bleached their flesh to an almost translucent milky white, adding to their reputation as "the milk-fed veal of game fish." The dinner is preceded by the much photographed eyeless fish round-up in which members of the volunteer fire department wrangle schools of the ghostly fish up the subterranean river to the antique fish weirs where the appropriately sized specimens are speared for the catch and the fingerlings allowed to return to the inky depths. The fry itself takes place in specially converted Airstream trailers, and the dinners are eaten alfresco on picnic tables constructed from southern Indiana hardwoods. The unseasoned bread-battered fillets of fish are served with the head as garnish and dipped in tartar sauce made from mayonnaise imported from the Trans-Indiana Mayonnaise Pipeline. Side dishes include potato, macaroni, and pea salads, though the purist accompanies the dish simply with a crustless slice of white bread dipped quickly in the boiling deep fat rendered from Hoosier hogs. Games that accompany the feast, most employing variations of blindfolding, include pin the eye on the fish and blindman's bluff, as well as a piñata-like game in which children, while hooded, whack a papier mache fish in hopes of breaking open the prize of glass marbles stuffing.

World Headquarters
KokomoKola Korp.
Kokomo

Founded in 1876 by a group of Union veterans who first tasted root beer and sarsaparilla captured from Confederate troops while campaigning in the South during Sherman's siege of Atlanta and subsequent march to the sea, KokomoKola Korp. has manufactured its own brand of successful soft drink ever since. Advertised as "The Refreshment That Gives Pause," KokomoKola continues to be the world's best-selling soda pop, made with carbonated milk and a secret formula of fat soluble ingredients known only to the five surviving descendants of the founders. The headquarters building and original bottling plant on US Highway 31 north of the city is open for visitors daily. At the end of the guided tour there is a tasting room where guests sample a wide selection of the company's product line including its skim and 2-percent lines, as well as its vanilla, colby, and ranch-flavored varieties. Nearby is the gift shop stocked with the famous proprietary merchandise, both antique reproductions and contemporary limited editions, including the rare Milk of Magnesia six packs and a few precious examples of the delicious Galax-ola special reserve label produced each spring with carbonation imported from the Pluto Spring (If Nature Can't Pluto Will!) of French Lick, Indiana. Leave an additional hour, at least, to explore the adjacent park grounds and farm yards landscaped by the architect Michael Graves, and featuring a series of milk fountains and a playful (though tame) herd of rare Dexter cows. There is punting, too, upon the vast holding ponds where the microscopic colonies of sweet acidophilus bacteria are nurtured on organic matter syphoned from the White River.

TRAVEL ADVISORIES

The World's First Parking Lot
Plato

In 1895 (six months after Elwood Haynes demonstrated, in a Kokomo test run, the first mechanically successful, self-propelled, clutch-driven automobile with electrical ignition and internal combustion gasoline engine), Hornus Barnett had an idea which, he would later record, came to him in a dream. With his younger brother, Willard, Hornus spent the next several days clearing the hydrangea, bridal wreath, peony bushes, and hollyhock from the side yard of their mother's green grocery on the outskirts of downtown Plato in anticipation of the earth-shaking consequences brought about by the invention of this new mode of transportation. The Barnett boys dubbed the 10-foot square of hard packed dirt, a result of multiple rollings with a device improvised by the boys from a pickle barrel and carriage tree, the "parking lot" and immediately applied for a patent which was granted after a protracted civil trial with competitors in Leominster, Massachusetts, in 1899. Within three months of the initial construction, the Barnetts introduced a further improvement, improvising the demarcation for the lot's two parking spaces with an application of crushed lime and quartz mica sprinkled along a straight line of staked baling twine. The brothers are also credited with the introduction of a whitewashed log to serve as a curb, indicating the stall's head-end boundary and preventing the accidental ramming of the store's side wall. After such an auspicious beginning, the contributions of the Barnetts to the further development of parking methods and technology declined as the brothers, divided over the more theoretical issue of "free" parking, quarreled, finally dissolving their partnership in 1902. Today, The World's First Parking Lot is preserved as a state historical monument and is included on the registry of significant engineering cites by Tau Lambda Delta, the engineering honorary. The two spaces are meticulously maintained, the striping reapplied immediately after rain or other inclement weather. However, visitors are urged to plan ahead. **Warning!** The Parking Lot Park, consisting of the 10-foot square lot and its surrounding parking lot which only accommodates up to 250 automobiles, is not equipped to handle recreational vehicles and bus tours, and is often at capacity early in the morning. When touring, plan for an early arrival and allow at least two hours for the visit.

The Federal Surface Materials Testbed
Highway US 31
Northbound and Southbound Lanes between
Rochester and Peru

Established by an act of Congress as part of the Defense Highway Bill of 1955, the Federal Surface Materials Testbed project extends for 25 miles between the cities of Rochester at the northern terminus and Peru at the southern one, with the town of Twelve Mile serving as the headquarters for the Corp of Engineers. Realizing President Eisenhower's dream of coast-to-coast driving without an intervening stoplight would demand extensive investment in the research and development of road-building techniques and space-age materials, Congress designated this segment of the US highway system as a practical laboratory to test the viability of a variety of surface agents *in situ* and in real-time. The lay motorist, then, plays a significant role when piloting his or her automobile at normal speed along this experimental corridor, contributing to the wear and tear of the competing materials which are also exposed daily to general weathering conditions. The 25-mile length of this unique laboratory is divided into 50-yard intervals of varying surface treatments. Concrete gives way to asphalt and then asphalt to cement. Macadam, tarmac, tar, oil mixed with pea-sized pebbles, black top, gravel, flagstone, wood plank, terrazzo, and compacted dirt, all are represented. The concrete genre alone deploys a vast array of these simulated stone surfaces. Composed of various adhesive media with aggregates of breccia, these amalgams are poured with devices improvised here and repaired with hot sealers of organic origin or synthetic fillers of latex or silicone. The substrata of the roadbed itself are composed of experimental materials and in as many different variations as the surfaces they support. Steel plates, used as temporary roadbeds nationwide, were first tested here, as were "Jersey" berms. And it was here that the optimum width of expansion joints in poured slabs was first realized and verified. Recently, several miles of the roadway have been given over to a priority fast-track task force investigation into the causes and the uses of potholes. **Warning!** Pay no attention to the signage along the right-of-way, since the informational and instructive messages, too, are only experimental in nature, testing the characteristics of durability and visibility in construction and color, and are, at the very least, misleading, if not downright dangerous, when heeded by the innocent motorist.

The Bermuda Triangle of Highway Travel
The Skip Wilkerson Freeway
The Calumet Region

In 1924, while piloting a modified Model A Ford on an aborted solo coast-to-coast non-stop land speed record attempt, Skip Wilkerson (barn-stormer, promoter of the second taillight, winner of the 1919 Logansport to Salt Lake Endurance Rally, and known in the press as the Lone Loner) disappeared near Hobart in the Calumet Region, the first recorded incidence in a series of unexplained vanishings, bizarre mechanical failures, and anomalous climatic phenomena concentrated in the northwest corner of the state. The dual lane memorial highway, constructed by the Civilian Conservation Corps in the summers of 1933 and 1934 during which 17 workers drowned when their transport truck sank in 12 feet of quicksand outside Portage, has continued to witness an ever-expanding history of mysterious accidents and/or extraterrestrial interventions in the region's vehicular traffic flow. Between the moment of the Lone Loner's disappearance and the inaugural ribbon cutting by Governor Norbert Schram (who died in the Triangle five years after the opening festivities when his hail-riddled, chauffeur-driven Auburn plunged into Hart Ditch during a July Fourth parade), no fewer than 168 other such occurrences were logged by The Regional Automobile Council, one of the first metropolitan governmental units in the country, established to investigate the burgeoning backlog of unsolved mayhem. The more famous cases have now become part of the national folklore, including the mysterious disappearance of a convoy of seven jeeps en route to the Great Lakes Naval Training Center, a school bus of Merrillville high-school band members who found their instruments could not be tuned once they transversed Munster, and the oft repeated anecdote of the accommodating trucker, a possible ghost, who gives lost hitchhikers a lift to the Highland Diner. **Warning!** Contemporary drivers are cautioned to use discretion when entering the region if they must. Tune car radios to 640 on the AM dial for weather updates and road conditions. A CB radio is advised as well as is an onboard GPS navigational system where available. Filing a travel itinerary with AAA or the Chicago Motor Club may very well save one's life.

The Gateway to the Cross Highway
Monon

While numerous highways and intersections nationwide have, along their grassy shoulders, the occasional display of a whitewashed hand-made cross, sometimes accompanied by a spray of faded plastic flowers to memorialize the site as the location of a fatal vehicular accident, State Road 16, heading due west to the Illinois line, far exceeds, in number and ambition, the construction of such roadside shrines elsewhere in the country's highway system. No fewer than nine hundred thousand separate crosses line the road, according to the Indiana Department of Transportation (IDOT), into whose jurisdiction general maintenance of the highway falls, creating an amazing and moving display as one motors over the level glacial plane toward the daily setting sun. The day-to-day upkeep of such a display and the constant insertion of new memorials is a daunting task. In light of that fact, the roadway is divided into mile-long segments and each segment administered in partnership with nearby local and civic-minded service or benevolent societies, such as church groups, fraternal or business associations, ladies clubs, the 4-H, scouting councils, and veterans organizations who volunteer to maintain, through general policing of litter and the routine lighting of the votive candles, the respectful integrity of what is now known as The Cross Highway. Of course, the thousands of crosses here displayed do not all represent local traffic altercations but seek to dramatize the total number of Americans killed in or by cars over the last fifteen years. The road is, therefore, highly touristed by loved ones seeking to visit the individual cross representing their personal loss. **Warning!** There is a statistical anomaly, duly represented by crosses, of a higher than average number of fatal accidents which do occur west of Monon along The Cross Highway. This elevated statistic of fatalities is attributed to the distractive nature of the cross display, its contribution to road fatigue and its accompanying loss of control, or, perhaps more likely, to the attractive nuisance the memorial drive projects to the disturbed mind, which invites vehicular suicide at speed, an expression, sadly, of the demented desire to end one's life amongst a copse of crosses, a premonition, in whitewashed wood, of one's own demise.

The Renomination Guerrilla Insurgency
I-69
From the Michigan border to Fishers,
North of Indianapolis

While in recent years the incidents of sabotage and am-
bush seem to have been quelled by the mobilization of three
companies of mechanized cavalry of the Indiana National
Guard, this might merely reflect the success of the ongoing
news blackout imposed by the state and federal governments concerning such activity. There are reports still of
sporadic hostile action along the 150-mile length of this
contested superhighway, leaked to the media by the insur-
gents' political wing. Escalating from peaceful demonstrations beginning in the early 1970s opposing the sexually
suggestive numbering affixed to the roadway, confrontation between transportation authorities and a militant fac-
tion of protesters composed of religious and civic improvement organizations soon turned violent after the collapse
of talks being held in Reykjavik, Iceland. Fuelled by oppo-
sition to the popularity of the interstate trucking
community's use of Citizen Band radio transmissions that
often employed off-color references to the interstate's nu-
merical designation, the confrontation reached its climax
with the Sturgis Affair. The family of seven, from
Muskegon, Michigan, en route home after vacationing in
Florida, became disoriented when, as a result of resistance
activity, all of the highway markers and junction indicators
were masked by burlap sacks. A massive air and ground
search and rescue operation was initiated once the Sturgises
were reported overdue by worried neighbors. Found alive
but severely dehydrated and badly shaken in a bombed-out
rest area near Pokagon State Park, the family, their car's
odometer on the fritz, had traveled back and forth along the
highway for days making illegal U-turns, once their confi-
dence as to their direction and distance toward their destination gave out. President Gerald Ford, touring the area in
1975, came under fire near the Garrett exit by a cadre of
renomination partisans who seemed indistinguishable from

the civilian population assembled to greet the dignitaries. Three in the entourage were wounded, including the Lieutenant Governor, Velma Smally of Noblesville. Bob Hope, in his last USO Christmas appearance, entertained the troops at the marine firebase near Upland. A marker commemorates that performance. **Warning!** As long as the Department of Transportation continues to support the appellation of I-69 to this stretch of the Interstate System, it is reasonable to assume agitation by the militant wing of forces engaged in this conflict of attrition will continue, thus making it incumbent upon the motorist to take care. The government has been unable to provide convincing assurances that any one section of the route is secured at any one time, as the fortunes of the conflict ebb and flow. Be prepared for spontaneous helicopter insertions, long range mopping up sorties led by elements of the 82nd Airborne, or annual summer mine countermeasures which might result in lane closings, detours, or speed restrictions. **Expect delays!** Pairs of Humvees (highly maneuverable, lightly armored troop transports built in South Bend, Indiana) continue picket duty along the median strip. One heading north, the other south, in order for their drivers to remain in close communication and ready for immediate action, the vehicles are deployed at close intervals over the entire length of the road.

THE SPORTS TOUR

Grand National Locomotive Drag Racing Finals
Whiting

Gone is the era when the crack streamliners of the Penn-sylvania and the New York Central cruised between Chicago and New York. In those days, the premier all-Pullman Limiteds (The Broadway and the 20th Century) would stage nightly races, emerging from the train sheds and terminals of the Windy City's Loop and then speeding on into the gloaming Indiana prairie along their paralleling high iron straight-aways. The muscular K-4 Pacifics of the Pennsylvania and the sleek J3a Hudsons of the New York Central, their moaning whistles once ubiquitous in the dreams of the residents of Gary, their spent cinders and smoke ash settling on the drying laundry of the clotheslines of Hammond, now, sadly, are no more. Gone, that is, except for each fall when steam-locomotive enthusiasts from all over the world gather along the historic right-of-way to witness the annual Grand National gathering.

Sanctioned by the National Association of Locomotive Railroad Racing (NALRRR, for short), a thousand engines and their crews vie in over fifty classes based on wheel arrangement, tractive effort, and firebox grate area in this, the final venue of the steam racing season.

Here the steam fan may witness the Raymond Loewy designed T-1 4-4-4-4 duplex with a modified Belpaire firebox go head-to-head with a Union Pacific FEF-3 4-8-4, boasting a static exhaust steam injector driving the water pump and feeding the water heater. Watch as they break the beams of the electric eye with speeds of up to 120 mph.

In the articulated class, spectators witness clashes of the Alleghenies and Challengers, as well as the super-qualified Big Boys of the impossible mountain grades, contending with the segmented Garratts imported all the way from East Africa.

In the modified heats, the cowled and varnished 4-8-4 of the Southern Pacific Daylight and the Norfolk and Western J grace the ribbon of rail, deploying their colorful drag chutes after streaking along the quarter mile course.

S-2 Turbines and Jawn Henrys, Atlantics and Pacifics, Mikados and Mallets and Mogols, Ten Wheelers and tank engines roar along the lake shore, their sanders sanding and their whistles whistling.

Perhaps the best represented class is of the red hot hot-rod 4-4-0s, American pattern engines, where even the garage hobbyist with ten tons of coal and a willing fireman can highball with the likes of Old Number 999, the first steamer to break the 100-mph mark back in 1893 on the head end of the Empire State Express.

Curiosities include the funny cars of the Erie's Triplex 2-8-8-8-2, B&O Camelbacks, geared Shays Loggers, and cab-forward oilers.

A special treat is watching the watering trails as crews compete at sluicing water on the fly, using a special scoop beneath their centipede tenders to refresh the tanks without stopping.

The colorful and noisy meet lives up to the famous bellowing of Hoosier AM radio djs who tout the race repeatedly:

"You think you can, you think you can, you think you can be there!"

With any luck you'll see a boiler blow.

Eugene V. Debs Memorial Pro-Am Golf Tournament
Terre Haute

A PGA-sanctioned event held each May Day at the Hulman Links north of the city, this three-day match play routinely draws the most competitive players on the tour as well as the largest gallery west of Augusta.

The Trent Jones-designed course is known for its stands of mottled sycamores, its hand-scythed fairways, its innovative use of the Wabash River, its ground-brick bunkers, and its excruciatingly difficult running dog-leg of the 7th hole.

The award of the coveted red jacket to the tourney's winning amateur is considered the ultimate prize for non-professional play.

Commemorating an obscure local politician, the "Debs," as it is affectionately known, commemorates the great American invention of the weekend while it also perpetuates the unique tradition of being the only professional venue on the world tour where the use of a caddy is strictly prohibited.

The 24 Hours of Indy
The Beltway
Indianapolis

Not as famous as The Indianapolis 500 or the Brickyard 400, the 24 Hours of Indy is, nevertheless, one of the premier events in motor-sports.

One Sunday each fall, the 106-mile beltway encircling the capital city is closed for this endurance test of Midget class front-engine roadsters. The continuous racing takes place on the inner lanes of I-465 while the outer lanes are reserved for the massive blocks of hastily constructed box seats and bleachers packed with racing's most rabid fans.

Averaging speeds of nearly 70 miles an hour, the Midgets complete the circuit in a little over an hour, thereby giving the spectators ample time between laps to socialize, picnic, and watch the race they are attending on portable televisions while perched upon what is often up to twelve stories of scaffolding. The various office buildings clustered at the highway exit ramps also offer great views as the pack of racers putter by below.

The 24 Hours of Indy is most notable for its unique pitting of its cars. As its course is, ordinarily, a public roadway and all remnants of the race are dismantled within two hours of its completion, the 24 Hours of Indy does not reserve a special area for repairs and refueling. In keeping with the endurance nature of the event, all servicing must be done while the cars are in motion. What have evolved are the justifiably famous rolling refueling trucks that also roam the course, searching for the running-on-empty racer. Docking, at times, with up to three cars by means of an elaborate winching system of hoses and accordion-like collapsing cranes, the fuel trucks themselves participate in their own contest of speed and endurance, a race within a race.

Occasionally, this risky maneuver at speed goes awry. The coupling which locks the hose to the tank springs free while the fueling is in progress. When this happens, the nearby stands of observers, who just moments before felt themselves lucky to be witnessing this fragile mating, now find themselves drenched in a spray of the highly flammable nitro-based racing petrol. Drivers who have followed in the wake of such an accident report witnessing thousands of people in whole segments of the bleachers ripping off their clothes, pouring from the stands naked, and running to bathe in the nearest insurance company's picturesque reflecting pond.

Home of the "Jeffersonville Slapper"
Louisville, Kentucky

It is a little known fact that the famous "Louisville Slugger" wooden baseball bat, manufactured by Hillerich & Bradsby, is actually produced in workshops located in Jeffersonville, Indiana, opposite the bat's namesake city, on the other side of the Ohio River. Almost as obscure is the intelligence that the equally famous "Jeffersonville Slapper," the preferred stick of the stars in the World Wiffle Ball Convention and ubiquitous in the bat bags of amateur leagues as well, is extruded in the Plastco factory found in Kentucky's largest city south of the river.

Recognizable in either its orange or yellow simulated wood grain configuration with its barber-pole black electrician's tape handle wrapping, the "Slapper" has been employed by such Wiffle legends as Warren Zahn, Simca Sanchez, Mildred "Babe" Hunsinger, and Franz Lidz, the home-run king and 1996 MVP, whose autographed version of the mass-marketed 38" model is a favorite with so many aspiring boys and girls.

As with its wooden cousin, whose selected ash dowels are a product of first growth forest of the Nancy Hanks National Park, the "Slapper" is also the result of the careful selection of raw materials and traditional American craftsmanship. Pellets of virgin vinyl arrive daily from the GE Plastics plant in Schenectady, New York, where they are melted in furnaces fueled by coal-bed methane tapped from the hill country of West Virginia, and formed by diamond dies cut by descendants of German immigrants from the Ruhr Valley.

Tours are available daily which conclude with a visit to the Plastco Outlet where the whole range of plastic sporting goods (ball gloves, helmets, protective cups, balls of all styles, apparel, proprietary paraphernalia, and non-cancerous non-toxic polyurethane simulated "chawin'" tobacco and snuff) is available for purchase. Or the visitor may attempt a session in the WWBC practice cages where it's "batter up!" all day long. One is welcome to take a few swings at pitches delivered from machines engineered to simulate the 3-meter sinker of Juan Nesbitt, the 12-mile-an-hour fastball of Thad, "'A' Train," Beber, the underhand knuckler of Gracie Pine or simply watch in awe as an errant wind catches a heater, which mimics the behind the back toss of Rod Maliszewski and suspends it, for a second or two, above the green cellulose bluegrass.

The Jefferson Proving Ground Gun Club
Jefferson Proving Ground

During the recent decommissioning of federal military installations, the sprawling Jefferson Proving ground, an army ordinance testing range in Jefferson, Jennings, and Ripley counties, was donated to the town of Wirt. Inspection of the property by the local populace yielded the disappointing intelligence that, after over 100 years of weapons testing on site, a civilian use for the area would be difficult to implement. Unexploded ordinance of all types littered the tree-denuded valley of the Muscatatuck River.

Initial plans for an international airport serving Holten, Dabney, New Marion, and Versailles had to be scrapped as did the ambitious hope for a free trade zone specializing in the importation and warehousing of spent nuclear fuel rods, asbestos lagging, and lead pipe. Happily, the imaginative townspeople of Wirt, led by their mayor Alberta Neville, conceived of a use conducive to infrastructure already in place. Now in its third year of operation, the Jefferson Proving Ground Gun Club is the world's only non-military skeet and trap facility exclusively designed for the discharge of large-bore firearms and artillery.

The club is able to provide ample target practice, both stationary and kinetic, for a wide variety of weaponry. Rifled cannon, howitzer, mortar, triple A, recoilless rifle, and Gatling gun can all be easily facilitated. At the pro shop one may find, for purchase or for rental: 88's; 105's; 155's; 2 inch, 3 inch, 5 inch, even 16 inch land or sea batteries; 20mm antiaircraft; 40mm antitank; quad fifties; Bofors guns, Oerlikon guns; bazookas, all kinds of shoulder mounted arms (both wire and laser guided); self-propelled grenades; and rocket launchers. The sportsman may deploy ammunition including antipersonnel or depleted uranium armour piecing, cluster bomblets, flack, and shrapnel as well as high explosive and incendiary rounds. The club even has several antique heavy cannon mounted on railway carriages which lob shells from the B&O siding at Wirt over to ground zero at Nebraska 25 miles away.

Once again, thanks to the heavily used facilities at the gun club, the students at nearby Hanover College can change classes in time with the tempo of exploding shells, feel the vibration of the landing rounds through their feet as they did before privatization, when the gunners of the U.S. Army were pulling the lanyards.

TEN LITTLE ITALIES OF INDIANA

1. The Knights of Columbus Hall
Columbus

Settled by Bakunin anarchists fleeing Boston in the wake of the Sacco and Vanzetti trial, the Italian community of Columbus stealthily blended in with the Hoosier natives of this town by dyeing their hair blond and changing all family names, en masse, to "Streeter". They emerged 70 years later from behind the many folds of secrecy (garlic, for example, was cultivated in various basements by means of full spectrum lighting and early experiments in hydroponic gardening) to take their place in the rich ethnic tapestry that is contemporary Columbus. The construction of the Knights of Columbus Hall marked the Streeters' proud return to ethnic identity. Taking full advantage of the noblesse oblige of local business giant Cummins Engine, which provides architectural fees for any civic building built within the town, the newly organized Knights commissioned Michael Graves to render their vision in a postmodern meeting hall located near the Philip Johnson Mason Lodge and the Frank Gehry Third African Methodist Episcopal Church. Immediately recognizable by the hermaphrodite xebec rigging of the faux nautical "sails" (really campanili) embroidered with red Spanish crosses, the hall quotes, architecturally, the nautical superstructure of the club's namesake's smallest vessel, the Nina. The cavernous Bingo Hall hosted the Bingo World Series in 1987 and again five years later in 1992. A mild hybrid of garlic, out of tradition, is still cultivated in the basement.

2. Camouflage Fashion Center
Milan

Settled by Carabiniere of the Italian alpine troops of the
Second World War after their release from POW camps at
Fort Benjamin Harrison, Milan (pronounced MY lan) supports a thriving apparel industry specializing in the production of camouflaged garments. It was in the workshops
and lofts of Milan that such famous sartorial patterns of
deception as "Northern European Snow," a white rip-
stopped gabardine splotched with daubs of gray and black,
and "Arab Chunk Cookie Dough," made famous during
the Gulf War, were developed for the military. The domestic outdoorsman market also benefits from Milanese designers' keen eyes. A stunning innovation was the recent
development of the bright safety-orange hooded synthetic
twill sweatshirt which still incorporates the patented outline of disrupting dazzle splashes in cinnabar-tinted umber
and incarnadine-influenced sienna. With runway seasons
both in fall and spring, the houses of Milan display their
creations for buyers who flock to this small Indiana town
to catch the first glimpse of these new interpretations of
light and natural habitat. There, to the beat of marshal
music, one might witness the introduction of such fabrics
as "Gray Grid," a distorting plaid that defeats the images
generated by star scopes and night-vision goggles or "Baby-
flage," a line of waffle-weave pajamas, sleepers, night gowns,
onesies, and long johns decorated with a woodland array
of primary colors which allows an infant to fade into its
toy-rich background.

3. The Purdue University Italian Sandwich
Research Kitchen and Sub Shop Experiment Station
Amo

Settled by shoemakers from Brindisi, Amo is now the home
of Purdue University's Italian Sandwich Research Kitchen
and Sub Shop Field Experiment Station. Here, new recipes

for flavored cheeses and spiced meats, originating in the experimental food laboratories of the West Lafayette campus, are tested in a variety of combinations and with a myriad of condiments and toppings upon an eager volunteer lunch population. Of interest is the extensive collection, displayed and mouth-wateringly preserved in the main building's lobby, of regional species of the genre, collected during class trips by the local 4-H. Under glass and neatly labeled are examples of the *Italian* of the Southern Midwest, the *Italian Sandwich* and the *Small Italian* of Southern Maine as well as the *Sub*, the *Submarine*, the *Hoagie* of Delaware Valley, the *Trunk*, the *Grinder* of New England, the *Bomber* of upstate New York with its distinctive layer of coleslaw, the *Atomic Rod*, the *Wedge*, the *Herk*, the *Blimpie*, the *Cuban Sandwich* of Miami, the greater and lesser *Po'Boy* and *Poor Boy* of the Delta, the *Zep*, the *Stromboli*, the *Mario*, the rare *Meatless*, the *Urp* and the *Grilled Urp*, the *Weasel* and the *Hot Wombat*, the *Podburger* of Omaha, the *Montegolfer*, the *Whole Toledo*, the *Torpedo*, the *Hero*, the *Anchovy Anaconda*, and last but not least the local *Last*, named for the foot-long blocks of wood, lasts, used by cobblers to mold leather for shoes.

4. The Grotto of Our Lady of Krylon
Churubusco

Settled by immigrants from Queens, New York, Churubusco is the site of the first appearance, west of the Alleghenies, of graffiti (a free-hand red tag, "RR123," affixed to a dust bin behind Kinze's Hardware Store downtown) on Pentecost Sunday, 1979. Churubusco was also the site, that same year, of the subsequent visitation in one of Oscar Yoder's soybean fields of the Virgin Mary, arrayed in a pastel disco-inspired raiment, instructing Oscar's son, Oder, that believers should protect and nurture all writing on walls. It fell to Father Johnny Raucci, pastor of St. Pat's, to begin construction of a shrine, still being built, commemorating the miracle and perpetuating the Mother of God's imperatives.

The Grotto employs in its facades a mosaic design made up of a variety of empty aerosol lacquer cans imbedded in stucco walls covered already with layers of spray painted inscriptions reaching a depth of two inches on some exterior surfaces of the basilica. It is here that Cardinal Primo Casaburo stopped briefly on his second tour of North America to try his hand with a yellow "Kilroy Was Here" in the narthex. Among the Grotto's many relics is a color Xerox reproduction of the Shroud of Turin, a synthetic stone cast of Lord Byron's scratched signature taken from the Temple of Poseidon at Sunian, Greece, which itself shows multiple defacement, and the scorched metacarpal and distal phalanx of the index finger of Saint Stencil of Trans Alpine Gaul, patron saint of vandals and sackers.

5. The Leaning Tower of Paoli
Paoli

Settled by refugees from the Kingdom of the Two Sicilies after an abortive attempt to integrate with the second utopian experiment at New Harmony, Indiana, Paoli (named for the Corsican patriot, Pasquale de Paoli, who led the struggle for independence from Genoa) is notable also for the famous leaning tower. The fifty-foot tower (actually an abandoned wood stave barrel tank once used by the L&N railroad to water steam engines when Paoli served as a division point and coaling station on the Louisville to Chicago sub-mainline) took on its characteristic 3-degree cant when wooden joists of one of its four support pylons were pilfered (after the tank was no longer used) in an abortive parquet bread board scheme of the mid 1950's. The citizens of Paoli, refusing to demolish the local landmark, instead buttressed the weakened legs with hydraulic jacks which over-corrected the initial tilt and left the structure at its current angle. The Italianate tromp l'oeil column was added during the Johnson administration to commemorate the visit of the First Lady, Lady Bird Johnson, during her promotion of a national beautification project. The tower, used today mainly as a test platform upon which high-school physics students from around the state recreate the gravitational experiments of Galileo Galilei, is known as one of the Seven Wonders of Indiana.

6. Old World Lawn Ornaments
Loogootee

Settled by the descendants of Carrara masons (lured to this country during the heyday of the booming limestone construction materials business), the artisans of Loogootee, for years, dressed and finished stones quarried for such famous buildings as New York's Rockefeller Center and the Empire State Building. With the decline of the stone industry after the Second World War, the Loogootee shops turned their talents to the fabrication of life-sized, painted and unpainted lawn statuettes and figurines sculpted in slag limestone gleaned from the abandoned quarries. Loogootee pieces, their subjects caught in the readily identifiable naturalistic style of the local studios, and posed in characteristic gestures of wide-eyed frenetic action or deep doe-eyed contemplation, are found on the finest lawns of North America (including the Reagan Ranch in California, the American Gothic House in Eldon, Iowa, and throughout Colonial Williamsburg and Henry Ford's Greenfield Village). In New York City, one may view the Henry Moore-inspired cherubic bunny series in the permanent collection of The Museum of Modern Art as well as the famous assemblage of Jockeys on the front porch of "21." Not to be missed: the annual blessing of the lawn ornaments at the Church of St. Francis which takes place during the patron saint's feast day in early October and coincides with the height of the region's fall foliage splendor.

7. The Only Active Volcano in the State
Mount Etna

Settled by Sicilians accustomed to living in the shadow of an active volcano, Mount Etna nestled at the foot of the 429-foot hill shelters several dozen families still engaged in the traditional peasant occupations of their forbears. There, on the fertile slopes of Mount Etna, the entire national crop of anise is cultivated each fall. Also in production are gourmet table grapes and raisins hybridized for use in chocolate-covered confections. The region's groves produce the specialty salad olive, a variety, due to the tendency of its fruit to break apart or split upon ripening, ideal as an ingredient in a green lettuce salad. Mount Etna, currently erupting particulate ash and steam, has attracted a colony of landscape painters who come to the area to employ what has been called the "Hoosier Light" in oils and watercolors to accent their renderings of the summit's brooding romantic nature.

8. The Ruins of Rome
Rome City

Settled by the families of extras appearing in the films of the Italian Neo-Realist Cinema who emigrated when the world-wide interest in such movies waned in the face of the French New Wave and Japanese samurai productions, Rome City today still retains some of the feel of the old country in the wake of Allied bombing, peopled by malnourished and homeless displaced persons. As if caught in time, the crumbling facades are just that—facades—lovingly recreated by the sentimental inhabitants and last employed by the entertainment industry as settings for the *Combat* television series of the 1960's. Each summer, the city holds its annual *Bicycle Thief* Days which features midnight showings of the movie, viewed by an audience, enthusiastically dressed as various members of the film's cast, that talks back to the screen, reciting, verbatim and in chorus, huge chunks of dialogue while weeping profusely.

9. The Canals of Chain O'Lakes
Chain O'Lakes State Park, Wawaka, Altona, Syracuse, Largo and environs

Settled by Venetians who had been recruited to complete, secretly, the Wabash and Erie canal after the canal's—and the state's—bankruptcy and collapse last century, in the face of emerging railroad competition, the Venetians today operate a clandestine transportation network of water-borne cargo, which extends throughout Indiana and on into all the cities and states of the Ohio River watershed and Great Lakes basin. The public waterways are awash with these "Liquid Gypsies" employing slow moving pontoon catamarans, bass boats, cabin cruisers, inboard family runabouts, canoes, sunfish, and inflatable dinghies to move their enormous contraband. It is said that theirs is a floating metropolis. Business is conducted by means of buoyant two-story diving ramps on the choppy waters of Lake Wauwausee. Biology and English classes of the public high schools are taught on lashings of drifting inner tubes meandering along the Mississinewa. The solemn ritual of extreme unction is performed by wet-suited priests on natant, paddle-powered funeral parlors wafting placidly along the Eel. These Venetians, as were their Old World ancestors, are famous for their hand-made glass. At night along the rivers and canals, the viaducts and mill ponds, one may observe the deep red fires of their furnaces reflected in the water. There: the sudden glowing expansion, the twinkling of fireflies, as the molten glass is blown into globes used as floats to suspend gossamer drift nets that dredge the channels for river perch, carp, pike, blue gill, and catfish.

10. The Littlest Little Italy
Fort Wayne

Settled by Antonio Martone who, at seventeen years of age, fled the influenza outbreak of Naples in 1919 and the real possibility that he would spend the rest of his life as a streetcar motorman, who got off the train at Fort Wayne thinking he had reached his original destination of Chicago, and stayed, living the rest of his life at 322 Brandriff Street, right behind the Nickel Plate roundhouse, where, at the same location ten years later, he opened an Italian grocery offering imported cheeses, meats, olive oils, pine and hazel nuts, and wines, as well as produce grown in his own backyard, such as plum tomatoes, basil, chard, pole beans, spinach, sweet peppers, and okra, along with the noodles he would roll out in his basement assisted by his wife, Madeline, who was brought from the old country, their marriage brokered by relations in Chicago, and who was Antonio's only customer for years at the store, running a tab she never paid and he never expected she should pay, and where they would sit in the kitchen drinking mineral water, grappa, and coffee, and eating, occasionally, Madeline's famous chocolate cake and where, also, they raised three children, a boy, Junior, and two girls, Mary and Carmella, who learned a little of the language and married Americans and moved away from where their parents would never move after moving so far away from their own birthplaces, and who would never leave again from Brandriff Street, listening to the trains whistling to each other in the yard while they themselves worked in their garden, where they also listened to the lilt of the neighborhood kids playing, riding their bikes up and down the cinder alley, making fun of the sing-song Italian accents made by the old couple by picking up the accent from the Martones working in their garden, shouting to each other as they worked, making fun of the foreigners and their language, naturally, but also finding, in what was left of it, a curious beauty that tasted strange and sweet on their young tongues.

ELI LILLY LAND

Editor's Note: Over the last several years, an Indianapolis drug company has been quietly purchasing a wide swath of swamp land and marginally profitable farms near the town of Martinsville. Recently, this bucolic setting has been transformed by a prodigious collection of construction equipment—earth movers and cranes, dump trucks and bulldozers—as the pharmaceutical giant breaks ground for an unprecedented new project opening in the spring of the year 2003:

Eli Lilly Land

A theme park whose theme celebrates the wonderful transformational and restorative powers of modern medicinal chemistry as well as the visionary genius of Eli Lilly—Hellenophile, philanthropist, historian, archaeologist, art connoisseur, botanist, husband and father, and inventor of the gelatin capsule—is designed for the whole family's entertainment and is promoted as being, at once, both thrilling *and* educational. Plans for the park, on the drawing board since the early 1950's, call for a magnificent six-square miles of meticulously maintained and manicured grounds, staffed by several thousand white-coated men and women—accurately referred to as "Lab Techs"—who will supervise the vast array of rides, prepare the sumptuous repasts at the Land's gourmet restaurants and drug store soda fountains, and assist the visitors with their purchases of souvenir pharmaceuticals and personalized pill boxes. And what would a theme park be without a cadre of costumed characters to conduct the visitors through the seemingly endless maze of entertainments and to pose with the delighted children for pictures? Graduated Cylinder; Mortar and Pestle; Dram Man; Eliot Narc; The Corpuscle Family; The Ether, and Doctor Doctor, MD; all of the favorite characters from Eli Lilly Comics, which have been distributed free of charge to physicians' waiting rooms since the Great Depression, will come to life daily on the 189 miles of roads, bike paths, and garden walks of the park. From the Michael Graves-designed visitors center, where you complete your induction physical and fill out various liability release forms, to the nightly Parade of Wonder Drugs which features the famous chorus line of high-stepping white rats, a day at Eli Lilly Land promises all a kaleidoscope of psychedelic high times.

The Blue Guide to Indiana is fortunate in having been provided with the following intriguing glimpse into the future by the visionaries of Eli Lilly Land. Here are some of the attractions that will come to life in 2003.

The Placebotron

On this ride the very willing volunteers (as all the park's guests are referred to) are provided with readily chewable and sweet-tasting tablets and told by the Lab Tech strapping them into the coaster car that they have been given a safe sugar pill to ingest before being whisked away on a leisurely five-mile roller coaster trip. In reality everyone has been given a specially selected fast-acting psycho-stimulant to enjoy with the scenery.

The Organic Chemistry Bumper Cars

Unlike other bumper car amusements, the electric motors that propel these cars also generate a powerful magnetic field. The cars, painted as carbon, hydrogen, or oxygen proceed to crash into each other, sometimes energetically rebounding as the fluctuating charge causes a repelling reaction, but more often after the collisions, forming elaborate and elegant chains of organic compounds and, more rarely, even polyesters and esters when the occasional inorganic vehicle, a bright yellow sulfur say, is released into the comical chemical collision.

The Gelatin Capsule House of Horrors

The Gelatin Capsule you ride in proceeds to dissolve as you travel along a highly detailed and thoroughly accurate recreation of the alimentary canal. Thrills await as you cascade through the simulated mucus-covered rooms, sluiced from the pharynx to the esophagus to the stomach and on to the intestines, both large and small. You race against time and the prospect of untimely elimination, hoping that you will be, through the marvels of virtual reality and computer-generated animation, absorbed into *The Body's Bloodstream*, an entirely separate ride, and on your way to where you can do the most organic good.

The Inoculatron

Roll up your sleeves and say ahhh! While relaxing on your own overstuffed and hypo-allergenic chaise, you will be inoculated, both by needle and orally, with the newest live and dead vaccines derived from the most fashionable designer viruses. With any luck you will develop a mild infection on the spot and experience the simulated effects of an actual fatal disease, spiking fevers while stimulating your body's own natural defenses. Children must be taller than the 150 cc mark on the cartoon Graduated Cylinder guarding the amusement's entrance.

It's a Prozac World

The engineering wizards of Eli Lilly Land have created this charming attraction to suggest that we are all the same under the skin. Scores of life-like automatons, dressed in the native costumes of children from around the world, serenade the enchanted visitor ensconced upon a silently gliding cloud car. The songs penned especially for *It's a Prozac World* by Dr. Joyce Brothers and Phillip Glass are performed by The Boys Choir of Carmel and seamlessly lip-synched by the happy, highly animated animatronic minions.

The Possible Side Effects Funhouse

After volunteers ingest fast-acting pharmaceuticals, the decks are cleared for the hilarity of hallucination and physiological truth or consequences. This funhouse, made to look like a Victorian asylum, is the setting for eye-popping (it's been known to happen) metamorphoses. The mirrors here reflect actual but rapid weight gain and water retention! That black light effect is your own lymph system a-glow! The hair loss is temporary but complete and it might just grow back in another color altogether, a souvenier of your visit! The lethargy, impotency, weeping spells, cotton mouths, blindnesses, unexplained elations, delusions of grandeur, shingles, yeast infections, excessive ear wax, malodorous breath, memory lapses, multiple personalities— all are part of the games in store. Where conventional funhouses nail furniture to the ceiling to create the illusion of an upside down world, here a pill introduces you to the varieties of vertigo, dizziness, and total coma while attempting a cure for, say, your fear of flying. Beware the injunctions against operating heavy machinery while taking these drugs, since the funhouse alcohol slides at the end of your journey sometimes lead in their corkscrewing paths to the vast parking lot and to the door of your very own car or a car very much like your very own.

Trade Mark City

Visitors to *Trade Mark City* experiment with proprietary rights while attempting to patent ordinary or generic compounds, extracts, plants, animals, and even elements by giving them imaginary and unpronounceable catchy names. The letters "z," "x," "q," and "v" are rationed, as are the umlaut and the asterisk.

The JumboMax Theatre

Playing perpetually on the big screen is the captivating narrative of *Accidental Discoveries* which documents, through dramatic recreations, amazing discoveries which occurred accidently. Spills and chills. Petri dishes left out over night. Mislabeled bottles. High jinx with fire extinguishers. Notes tampered with to doctor the bell curve in a lab section. Lots and lots of stray electric charges including a famous one dealing with static electricity and the vulcanizing of rubber.

And last but not least...

The Amnesiac-a-tron

At day's end of this eventful visit, powerful anesthetics are administered by competent hands and the amused amusement park goer is eased into twilight sleep where flights of recording angels transcribe the babbling confessions of their truth-induced charges. One wakes refreshed and often minus one's wisdom teeth if one had them to begin with and is encouraged to read over and sign the documents of incriminating evidence which the Eli Lilly company will hold on file in case there is any future litigation resulting from one's visit to "the apparently happiest place you remember on what you think might be something called Earth!"

SCENIC WASTE DISPOSAL
AND STORAGE SITES

Field of Light Bulbs
Star City, Pulaski County

For the last quarter century, Indiana has served as a designated destination for various residential and commercial waste products emanating from urban and industrial centers located in other states. Various material including asbestos furnace duct and steam pipe lagging, medical and dental detritus, low-grade radioactive isotopes from obsolete smoke detectors, Christmas trees, motor oil, construction debris of all kinds, along with many other varieties of organic and inorganic refuse have found their way via rail, barge, or motor carriage to the spaces of the sparsely populated hinterlands of the state—abandoned farm fields, played-out quarries, shopping mall land-fills, and drained marshes—for final disposition.

Perhaps the most attractive and intriguing of these facilities is the Light Bulb Transfer Station located outside Star City. A field nearly one square mile, a little over 600 acres, or almost one whole section of Tippecanoe Township has become the exclusive final resting place for burned-out electrical illumination.

The Field of Light Bulbs, which approaches ten feet deep in certain places, is made up of lamps of all kinds. From a distance, the treeless and slightly undulating expanse strikes the visitor as a sparkling snow-covered field in the sunlight but, upon closer inspection, one may discern the crystalline

pointillism of individual incandescent bulbs and floods, fluo-
rescent tubes and coils, decorative frosted candles, miniscule
halogens, snaking neon piping, all accentuated by occasional seams of yellow bug lights, a smattering of diminu-
tive flashlight bulbs, automobile headlights and flashers,
or ultraviolet gro-lights.

The citizenry of Star City, sensitive to the negative aspect
of this, their village's largest private employer's industry,
while, at the same time, taken by the natural beauty and
unique feature of the facility, has made the site available to
the visitor by means of a meandering self-guided and inter-
active pressure-treated wood boardwalk skimming above
the top-most crust of mostly milky glass. Not to be missed
is the corner of the field where high tension power lines of
the Northern Indiana Public Service Corporation cross overhead. Here, the magnetic fields the transmission wires generate occasionally will illume a constellation of rogue fluo-
rescent fixtures which have inadvertently found their way
to obsolescence before their time. Also be on the look-out
for small bands of the colorful tungsten pickers, a local
caste of scavenger, who open up mines in the drifts of light
bulbs to reclaim the precious metal from within the spent
electric bulbs. Tell-tale evidence of their presence is the piles
of discarded socket screws left behind like shells on a beach
after a July 4th clam-bake.

The Mothball Fleet of Garbage Trucks
Beech Grove

To this suburb outside of Indianapolis come the retired garbage and trash hauling trucks declared as surplus or redun-
dant by municipal entities and sanitary districts nationwide.
Here, stripped of their more valuable electronic components,
gleaned of their hydraulics, drained of fuel and fluid, the
trucks' tires are removed and the remaining frames and bod-
ies are placed on blocks at sabotage-discouraging intervals.

The vehicles are prepared for indefinite storage in anticipation of future reactivation during expected, though undesirable, cartage emergencies. The retired trucks may also serve as sources for needed spare parts, cannibalized by skilled teams of roving technicians. The humid climate of these former soybean fields south of the capital city, provides a pristine environment for such mothballing, assuring a fleet of heavy duty trucks in a ready reserve.

Walking tours of the site are available, where the visitor will be amazed by the variety and ingenuity displayed in the handling of kitchen garbage, tallow, rubbish, ashes, sawdust, and trash of all description. More poignant are the remnants of decorative display such as cartoon characters, beloved names and names of beloveds adorning their air-brushed images, and scripts of catchy slogans applied to the cabs of the trucks by their zealous crews. "Litterbug." "Stuff It!" "Outta Sight, Outta Mind!" Stenciled along the flanks of fender after fender are icons representing countless missions performed. Here, affixed to a rust-specked grill by means of twist ties, the remains of a teddy bear or doll baby rescued from a bin. There, a playful hood ornament of an eight ball, cookie jar, or electric fan, handiwork of a bored driver stuck on line at the scales of some remote landfill. Picnic areas with cook stoves are scattered around the lots as well as latrines and potable water spigots, but note that the facility has no trash receptacles, and everything packed into the site must be brought out again by the hiker.

The State Hair Dump
Auburn

For close to two centuries it has been illegal to burn shorn hair within the state of Indiana. The enabling legislation of this statute may be found in an article of the state's constitution of 1815. The current active land-fill, the seventh in the state's history, in operation for the last twenty years, may be found off Indiana Highway 8 to the north of Auburn in Dekalb County.

The hair, exposed to the elements in an open pit, is kept constantly wet by means of massive overhead irrigating sprinkler system out of concern for lightning strikes and the careless camper, as well as to dampen the possibility of drifting fur during the gale conditions of the fall and spring. The native deciduous underbrush is kept constantly pruned, thus discouraging a conflagration of the type that engulfed the dump at Dugger during the Great Depression, burning, out of control, for seventeen months and contributing to, through the hazy smoke the fire produced, the Summer Without Summer of 1933.

Hair arrives at Auburn daily, collected from all over the state. A clipping begins its journey, usually, by being swept up immediately after the barber or beautician completes his or her operation, and the hair is whisked into specially marked galvanized bushel baskets, which are then collected into customized wooden carts drawn by Bernese Mountain dogs. The hair accumulates at regional distribution depots, where the state health department conducts random testing before it is transhipped in aggregate via glass-lined covered hopper cars, hauled by dedicated unit trains to the Auburn location.

Surrounding the hair dump are many beauty salons, barber colleges, and sundry hair stylists seeking to reduce their overhead by discounting the destination surcharge in the cost of the above mandatory shipping. Many customers, who may drive miles to employ the services of one or more of the local shops in close proximity to the dump, report a richer tonsorial experience being groomed within sight of the mountainous collection of hair and the ever-shifting light playing over the layered landscape.

There are several helicopter sightseeing services available to the visitor. At any moment, a dozen or more whirlybirds may be buzzing and hovering with their charges overhead.

World's Tallest Incinerator Smokestack
Richmond

Surpassed in the western hemisphere only by Toronto's CN Tower as the tallest, free-standing, man-made structure, the brick and steel smokestack venting the municipal incinerator at Richmond has, twenty feet from its top, a completely enclosed, climate controlled, two-story observation deck. Reached by means of a glass elevator which scales the smokestack's northern facing side, the observation deck provides the visitor with an unobstructed 360-degree view of farm fields in two states, Indiana and Ohio, when amplified, on a clear day, with coin-operated telescopes stationed around the platform.

Though a locally owned facility designed to incinerate the entire waste stream of north central Indiana and western Ohio, while co-generating steam which is then used in the production of electricity sold through the Midwestern Grid to the Tennessee Valley Authority, the facility's capacity makes it necessary to import the bulk of its combustible material from the eastern seaboard, many European countries, and all of Iceland. Managed, under EPA supervision, by a Japanese conglomerate, the incinerator is famous for its "bag room," an area the size of seven football fields, where the inevitable cinders and particulate ash left over from the burning process are filtered from the exhaust gases. The resulting amalgam is the primary ingredient in the plant's famous cinder-block product line which is exported to the building trades of Pacific Rim countries.

Sunset is a spectacular time to enjoy a trip to the airy perch atop the world's tallest smokestack. Just above your head

as you view the panoramic landscape, the scrubbed and
scalded effluent of the process far below microscopically
emerges as chains of harmless organic compounds, ozone,
and a mix of hydrocarbons laced with mere traces of sul-
phur or nitrogen on the wings of superheated inert air.
From the world's tallest smokestack the exhaust mingles
with the prevailing westerly wind. Lit by the retreating light,
the eastward spreading plume, which extends for miles, is
phosphorescent in the gloaming and can, when conditions
are right, create its own weather, which you may observe,
downstream.

THE SEX TOUR

Editors Note: The photographs that were to accompany this segment of *The Blue Guide to Indiana* were not available at the time this issue went to press. The editor heartily apologizes for this inconvenience and has been assured by the service bureau that said illustrations are coming forthwith. The reader who is curious about these missing photos is urged to write the editor at this address stating his or her desire for them and attach to this request a stamped, self-addressed, business-sized return envelope. Upon receipt, this publication will happily return a set of the intended photographs suitable for pasting into the article's body copy at the indicated areas. It will be necessary only for the reader to moisten the adhesive on the photographs' reverse with his or her tongue.

Archaeological Site of The Wauwausee Drive-In
Syracuse

fig. 1

Shown (figure 1), is the panoramic overview of the archeology dig, its trenches rigged with wire grid for photographic recording, of a drive-in theater outside Syracuse.

fig. 2

Also shown (figure 2) is a portrait of the French excavation team with their locally recruited Hoosier laborers. Prof. Hippolite Neff, in the pith helmet, of *Les etudes des Americans*, The Sorbonne, is the project director and the visionary guiding spirit behind the effort to locate the ornate lost movie amphitheater. Neff, disparaged by his European colleagues for his conviction that such entertainment precincts existed, treated evidence found in folk narratives as a reflection of historic fact and not literary imagination.

Here, in times gone by, moving images were cast upon gigantic luminescent screens which seemed to stimulate and sexually excite an audience ensconced in specially equipped automobiles arranged in fan-like patterns below the glowing pictures. The work of the French team has already demonstrated a sustained human presence on the site and has identified the charred remains of a foundation as a palisade enclosure which encompassed nearly five acres of land. At the very rich strata, identified by Neff as "6B," there is strong evidence of the conflagration alluded to in the folk narratives. This coincides, through carbon dating, with the sketchy historic record of the mysterious Daylight Savings Wars of 1948 and 1955 in which farmers of northern Indiana battled the proprietors of drive-in movies for the control of local time.

Many of the treasures uncovered have been quickly transferred for study and display at the Louvre and other museums in France and the Netherlands, but a significant collection of artifacts is available for public inspection, on site, at the reconstructed *"stand de concession,"* itself a marvel and a testament to Neff's energetic imagination. Shown below (figure 3).

fig. 3

An elegantly painted, multi-hued cinder block building, its walls pierced by glass doorways, suggests the rich aesthetic sensibilities of the drive-in *habitués*. One must remember that much of what went on here was in the dark, after all, or illumined by the weakest of yellow insect-repelling incandescent bulb lighting, here, lovingly restored. Within, there are displayed the shards of neon tubing and rusting sheets of galvanized metal which once sheathed the five-story tall screen upon which the movies were projected. Most significant are the fossilized remains of courtship rituals including petrified prophylactics, fraternity pins and lavalieres, chewing gum and straws which retain actual dentition marks, as well as the remnants of what the French team believes to be their most treasured find—period underclothing and foundation wear, constructed of unknown but seemingly indestructible synthetic fabrics.

The US Steel Condom Works
Burns Harbor

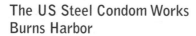

fig. 4

Shown (figure 4) above is an aerial view taken, in 1940, from the United States Navy Blimp *Akron* of the massive Burns Harbor facility where US Steel has manufactured latex and natural membrane prophylactics beginning before America's entry into the Second World War. During the Roosevelt administration's rearmament campaign anticipating Pearl Harbor, the industrial giant, already heavily invested in many Indiana cities throughout the Calumet Region, secretly purchased the 800-acre site in small, seemingly noncontiguous parcels. Overnight, it seemed, the sprawling complex sprang up from the arid dunes and fetid marshland of northwestern Indiana.

At the height of production, as the nation readied for D-Day and the liberation of Europe, the Condom Works manufactured nearly 2 million units per hour. Ingots of natural raw rubber imported from the Missabe Range plied the waters of the nation's inland seas, Lakes Superior, Huron, and Michigan, shipped on fleets of specially designed freighters, while finely milled corn starch from the Heartland arrived around the clock on mile-long, expedited trains forwarded from the Chicago, Burlington & Quincy, the Illinois Central, and The Rock Island via a special stub-end siding of the Chicago Belt Railway. The stockyards and slaughter houses, alone, were able to process 400 lambs a day at the same time the smelter and rolling mill rendered 6000 cubic yards of scrap aluminum ready for foil packaging. The Calumet River itself was diverted to a 17 billion gallon reservoir to service the plant's thirsty needs including the rigorous quality control program in which every fifth condom underwent hydroponic inflation. U.S. Steel's chemical unit also maintained an extensive presence here, developing a variety of spermicide and lubrication emollients, many still in use today.

From its heyday in the 1940's, the plant has sadly contracted, in the face of expanding foreign competition, high labor costs and the changing demands of the domestic market. In response to these pressures, U.S. Steel, in concert with the United Rubber Workers of America and the regional development authority, has launched an aggressive re-tooling at Burns Harbor, concentrating on innovative color application, synthetic substitutions, texture manipulation, and experiments with the XF100, a female version of the famous condom. Much of the floor space of the original factory has been converted to other uses, including related retail industries, or has been donated to the city and renovated for civic enrichment. The visitor today may choose between such venues as the factory outlet mall and the hands-on Carnegie Children's Museum of Science and Industry.

The So-So Smokey Mountain National Forest and The Hoosier Infidelity Resort Area Story

Designated a national forest in 1923 after an intensive lobbying campaign by the southern Indiana coal interests. In order to more easily log and mine the third growth timberland, dealing with an indifferent and absent federal landlord was preferred over an unpredictable conglomeration of individual landholders. The So-So Smokey Mountain National Forest is today known for its extensive system of "modesty strips"— bands of standing trees and bushy undergrowth left untouched along roadways—which then mask the clear-cut swaths of woodland harvested just beyond sight, giving the illusion of pristine and primeval forest. The annual autumnal Hoosier ritual of "going leaf-looking" takes on a certain poignancy when one realizes that the flaming yellow, red, and orange display of fall finery is, in fact, the handiwork of the lumber companies' exterior decorators, who extend the screening season of the hardwoods' leaves once the leaves have actually fallen by the application of artful camouflage. The blaze of color, carefully recorded by countless snapshots and video cameras, is due, more often than not, to the artificial leaves which now, to most, look more like fall foliage than the fall foliage itself.

The village of Story has been transformed, by its proximity to the National Forest, into a bustling resort similar to the vibrant areas at the gateways of other natural wonders, such as Gatlinburg, the Catskills, or Niagara Falls. But unlike those other resorts, made famous for their aggressive hospitality toward the newlywed, Story caters predominantly to couples engaging in adulterous trysts and surreptitious, squalid, and sultry affairs of the heart. Shown in figure 5, next page, Second Street, the town's main street, is lined with a myriad of seemingly cheap hotels, ramshackle motor-courts, vandalized tourist cabins, decaying boarding homes and flophouses, all illumined with a variety of sputtering neon and pulsing window signage.

fig. 5

The aura of general seediness is, however, an illusion. The squalid details of the facades are mere camouflage for the largest concentration of five-star hotels in the state. Within the sumptuously appointed suites, discreet couples will discover the famous A-shaped beds and baths of the region, as well as wet bars, ceiling mirrors, and an unlimited supply of towels. For the more adventurous, the town also offers alternative amusements, such as several wax museums and shops specializing in antique dress-up in disguise daguerreotype. Visitors will be pleased to note that matchbooks, postcards, and complimentary toiletries are scrupulously devoid of any geographic or telephonic addresses.

Contributing to the unique nature of the place and adding to its atmosphere of an exotic getaway is the genetic anomaly present in the native populace and first identified by researchers from The Johns Hopkins Hospital in 1931. A consequence of inbreeding and/or the indigenous artesian springs, Koy's Syndrome expresses itself as a chronic and specific dysfunction of the short term memory, and hence the inability to distinguish reality in stories either read or heard, as well as an irrational aversion to ingestion of legumes and the handling of paper money.

The Site of the First Observed Human Female Orgasm in America
Fort Wayne

Pictured below (figure 6) is the marker erected by the National College of Sex Researchers and Sex Therapists to commemorate the centennial of the first American observations of the human female orgasm by Dr. Joseph R. Beck at the home of his patient, Mrs. H. L____ , on August 7 and 8, 1872.

fig. 6

Dr. Beck first published his findings in the *St. Louis Medical and Surgical Journal* the following month and delivered the same paper to the American Medical Association two years later when an expanded version was published in the November 1874 edition of the *American Journal of Obstetrics and Diseases of Women and Children*. Mrs. L____ who was, at the time, thirty-two years old and living with her husband of eight years in their middle-class home on the corner of Spy Run and Tennessee Avenue, now the parking lot of a mortgage loan company, was suffering from a severe "falling of the womb" or retroversion of the uterus. When fitting her with a pessary offering mechanical support, Dr. Beck, having already observed his patient was "an intelligent and appreciative lady," also noted, in the course of the examination, signs of sexual arousal if not possibly orgasm. Dr. Beck continues:

> In making my visit to the residence of the patient the next day, for the purposes of adjusting the supporter, I made a second examination by

touch, and upon introducing my finger between the pubic arch and the anterior lip of the pro-lapsed cervix, I was requested by the patient to be very careful in my manipulations of the parts, since she was very prone, by reason of her ner-vous temperament and passionate nature, to have sexual orgasm induced by a slight contact of the finger, a fact which I believed had been manifested in my office examination of the pre-vious day, and which she afterward admitted having been the case. Indeed she stated further that this had more than once occurred to her while making digital examination of herself.

To Dr. Beck, the possibility of observing Mrs. L_____'s cervix while she actually experienced an orgasm was of the very greatest scientific interest. The raging medical controversy of the day centered on explaining how sper-matozoa entered the uterus from the vagina. A possible theory involved a sucking or aspirating action of the cer-vix as the principle conveyance. This was disputed by oth-ers. Mrs. L_____'s cervix was visible through her labia and hence offered Dr. Beck the opportunity to lay the con-troversy to rest.

Carefully, therefore, separating the labia with my left hand, so that the *os uteri* was brought clearly into view in the sunlight, I now swept my right forefinger quickly three or four times across the space between the cervix and pubic arch, when almost immediately the orgasm occurred, and the following was what was presented in my view—

Instantly that the height of excitement was at hand, the *os* opened itself to the extent of fully an inch, as nearly as my eye could judge, made five or six successive gasps, as it were, drawing the external *os* into the cervix each time powerfully, and, it seemed to me, with regular rhythmic action, at the same time losing its former density and hardness, and becoming quite soft to the touch. All these phenomena occurred within the space of some twelve seconds of time certainly, and in an instant all was as before. At the near approach of orgastic excitement the *os* and cervix became intensely congested, assuming almost a livid purple color, but upon cessation of the action, as related, the *os* suddenly closed, the cervix again hardened itself, the intense congestion was dissipated, the organs concerned resolved themselves into normal condition, and their relations to each other became again as before the advent of the excitement.

Dr. Beck's observation held sway for more than half a century finally being eclipsed by the work of Dr. Robert Latou Dickinson in 1949. Dr. Dickinson's use of a transparent glass phallus equipped with a headlight demonstrated that the inch-wide gasping entrance to the cervix was at best a rare and perhaps imagined phenomenon.

Dr. Beck's papers and surgical instruments are on display in the rare book room of the Dale McMillian Library on the campus of the Indiana Institute of Technology, Jefferson Boulevard.

The First Lovers' Lane™
Madison

The story is now familiar to most everyone—how Roy Crank, a Fuller Brush Man working the tri-state area, purchased a cul-de-sac on a bluff overlooking the Ohio River from the Swinney brothers—who had allowed the local youth access, in a random fashion, to their property for the purposes of late-night petting and necking in their automobiles—and who then sold the idea of romantic off-street parking, creating the most successful franchise system in the world. Shown (figure 7), the original Lovers' Lane™ was designated a state landmark by Governor Evan Bayh in 1993 and placed on the National Register of Historic Places.

fig. 7

The architecture of the nearly seven-thousand Lovers' Lane™ properties in the chain has changed over the years. The quaint details of the Swinney property have evolved to those immediately recognizable features of the modern corporate identity—such as the famous lavender Do Not Enter© signs—which now adorn Lovers' Lane™ outlets everywhere. Gone, now, are the elm trees and the yellow fifty-gallon drums, the "Senior Rock" with the layers of spray-painted graffiti and the sparkling landscape of glinting smashed amber glass, cigarette butts, and rusting cans. The preservation work at Madison has lovingly restored these unique features to create the nostalgic authentically 1950's original which is meticulously maintained and serviced by the students of the company's famous Kissin' Kollege®, whose campus is located nearby in Vevay. There, new franchise owners and manager trainees endure an intensive six-week orientation course in order to familiarize themselves with the company's product line and procedures, thus ensuring that Lovers' Lane™ industry-leading quality control standards are maintained.

A PARADE OF HOMES

The Will H. Hays Home and Library
Crawfordsville

A life-long party activist and Chairman of the Republican National Committee, Will H. Hays (a Crawfordsville native and attorney) was appointed postmaster general by President Warren G. Harding as a reward for Hay's support in Harding's successful presidential campaign of 1920. On January 14, 1923, Hays became the president of the Motion Pictures Producers and Distributors Association. There he proceeded to develop the codes member companies were expected to follow, thereby imposing industry self-censorship in place of that promoted by the growing number of decency leagues and religious denominations upset with the immoral excesses of industry personnel and its increasingly popular product. The house, in the Carpenter Gothic style, is conserved to replicate its appearance at the height of the Hays Commission. The period furnishings, restored by the local Junior League, have been augmented by personal mementos and souvenirs from the family collection, including a beanie once worn by Fatty Arbuckle, a matched set of gold-plated shears presented to Mr. Hays by Herbert Hoover, commemorative bars of soap inlaid with semi-precious stones and rare tropic woods (created by the Proctor and Gamble, and Colgate-Palmolive companies commemorating Mr. Hays's retirement), and the specially commissioned Oscar statuette awarded to Hays in 1935, the only Academy Award sculpted with all its clothes. There is always a fire burning in the adjacent library, which contains a King James version of the Holy

Bible signed by Billy Sunday, a Vulgate edition of Augustine's *Confessions*, an Illustrated Classics comic book of *The Song of Songs*, as well as the collected sermons of Father Coughlin and the largest collection of unmade motion picture scripts, film treatments, and synopses in the world. Here too, the Convention on American Slang maintains a maildrop and database monitoring the ever-changing field of euphemistic expression. The library converts to a comfortable screening room where risque trailers and quaint objectionable outtakes are occasionally shown to invited guests and visiting dignitaries. The stained glass windows look out upon the backyard garden and basketball court where, it is said, Commissioner Hays, deep in thought, walked on his way to the rustic outhouse, a two-holer in the Cotswald manner, screened by an impressive stand of lilacs.

The Bill Blass Birthplace
Fort Wayne

A plaque next to the front door of this modest bungalow attests to the fact that Bill Blass (one of this nation's premier designers and clothing manufacturers) was born in the back bedroom attended only by a midwife who performed an episiotomy (a result of a breech presentation), the stitching of which was the earliest memory of the newborn sartorial star. Stories are still told of his prodigious talent designing and sewing much of his own layette once he dismissed the prenatal collection of gowns and onesies as uncomfortable, impractical, and out of date. By two, with the aid of an apparatus for reaching the foot treadle of his mother's Singer (preserved and displayed at the birthplace) Bill, as he was known by the neighborhood, had already established a thriving custom alteration business, independently contracting tailoring services with the Patterson Fletcher Department Store downtown, as well as providing most of the south side of the city with coordinating window treatments, still evident to this day, in what would become his signature palette of colors and fabric. In high school, Blass provided the school mascot, the Archer, with an entire trousseau of tunics, hosiery, caps, capes and codpieces, along with the matching accessories of bow, arrow, and quiver. Examples of all this early work are represented in the birthplace's holdings, including the entire portfolio of drawings rendered for his junior prom, providing the evening ensemble for the entire class cotillion. Also on display at the birthplace, Blass-designed wallpapers, wall paint, carpet, area rugs, upholstery, toweling, napkins, flatware, perfume and toiletries, belt buckles, basketball uniforms and shoes, sunglasses, shoes, underwear, shower curtains, and stationery, examples of which are all available for purchase in the gift shop. An additional ticket is required to view the 1974 Ford LTD in navy blue pearl coat and taupe leather trim which is parked on the adjacent lot. The birthplace also possesses the most complete collection of timetables for the midwestern lines and routes of the Pennsylvania Railroad, a hobby of the young Bill Blass, which he passionately maintained and added to, up until the very moment of his own departure for New York City, on the Broadway Limited, the day after he graduated from South Side High School.

The Earl Butz Farm
Albion

Except for the interpretive center in the trailer of a North American Moving van, the Earl Butz Farm (the boyhood home of Earl Butz, Secretary of Agriculture under Richard Nixon) is now part of a larger, privately owned farm. The land itself, 400 acres in Sycamore Township, is currently the property of an Italian insurance company and is leased to the Big Mac Management Group, a subsidiary of Central Soya Industries, headquartered in Decatur. None of the buildings known to exist during the former secretary's childhood (two houses, summer kitchen, root cellar, storm cellar, mow barn and silo, tool shed, tractor shed, corncrib, coops, pole barns, pumphouse, springhouse, horse barn, grain bins, garages, green houses, mill, machine shop, manure tanks, cannery, warehouse, fuel bunker, loafing shed, pigpens, nursery and farrowing houses, child's play-house, woodshed, and outhouse) survives. Before the land is planted to corn or soy beans, it is possible, with a bit of imagination, to reconstruct the bare outlines of the domes-tic structures' footprints by using the small stands of rhu-barb and horseradish that somehow germinate each year to outline the buildings' lost foundations. One may easily discern the remains of the former dirt-floored basketball court, bordered by fox-tail and milkweed. There are the ruined and rusted struts of a windmill tower (the well be-neath it too deep to fill) that are used as a base station for the citizen's band radio employed by the seasonal fieldhands. There is not a fence nor fence post in sight, though the interpretive center has a collection of barbed wire. The fertile family graveyard, however, still yields, after all these years, a rich assortment of artifacts and hu-man remains which are freshly turned up each spring dur-ing spring field work by state of the art, 24-bottomed, mold board chisel plows. Agronomy experts from Purdue Uni-versity believe all indications are that such material will continue to be produced for, perhaps, several years more, as the topsoil is routinely eroded.

The Underground Levittown
Evansville

Terry Flynn had a dream. It came to him while he slept a quarter mile below the surface of the earth, on a cot, in a shack he constructed off the main bore of the #3 Bill Baer coal mine, where he worked during the waning months of the Second World War. His dream was of abundant affordable housing for the expected southern Indiana contingent of demobilized veterans and their new families. Flynn, along with many of his mining colleagues, had been working feverishly through the dark war years to extract the anthracite necessary to stoke the furnaces of wartime democracy. In order to save commuting time to the surface and to afford some protection from the tunnel's continuing flaking gneiss dust while having lunch or enjoying a cup of joe, the miners had rigged a series of comfortable shacks and shanties all the better to sleep, eat, bathe, and even relax, as many were equipped with radios, reading lamps, and the ubiquitous backboard and basketball hoop with net. Flynn's dream was to convert and expand these vernacular domestic expressions into a complete village of actual single-family dwellings, a true *sub*urban mecca beneath the streets of Greater Evansville. Terry Flynn's dream is, today, a thriving reality where over four-hundred families call the Underground Levittown, as it is known, home. The community boasts seven churches, a synagogue and a mosque, three movie theaters and a drive-in, several restaurants and coffee shops, a new mall, and a very active volunteer fire department. The town has its own post office with its own zip code, not a *sub*station of Evansville, topside. And the high-school basketball team placed second in last year's regional tournament. Husbands appreciate the low maintenance costs associated with living underground, as well as the constant 70-degree ambient air temperature. Their wives love the accessibility to abundant fresh produce, especially the specialty mushrooms and distinctive blue cheeses. And the children, secure in this gated community, explore the endless side tunnels and abandoned galleries and scrapped extraction equipment of this former mine, often excavating their own extensive tunnel systems beneath the scaled-down playhouses in their backyards. The visitor center is located immediately adjacent to the main elevator shaft where an extensive photo gallery records the evolution of the town's original identical salt-box tract housing into the individual expressions of domestic tranquility we see today, an extension of each homeowner's unique personal taste and disposable income.

Historic Colonial Virginia Sandidge Homestead
Madison

This two-story colonial style house and landscaped yard
on Elm Street is a living history museum where enthusiastic volunteers reenact the life and times of Virginia Sandidge
and her family of five (two girls and three boys) circa 1985.
Sandidge, who currently lives three doors down the street
in a three bedroom/two-and-a-half bath ranch house, is an
associate professor of English at nearby Hanover College,
where she instructs freshman in composition and occasionally teaches Chaucer to a small class of undergraduates.
Donated to the state in 1989 and administered in trust by
the Rockefeller Foundation, the Homestead provides a fascinating glimpse into everyday domestic existence from a
dozen years ago. Daily demonstrations feature the cast
member playing "Virginia Sandidge" (the single head of
household mother of five) preparing the daily "sack"
lunches for her children, including traditional peanut butter sandwiches and the careful distribution of Seifert potato chips into individual plastic bags. Visitors witness the
making of a pot of coffee, employing what, in 1985, was a
still novel appliance, the automatic drip coffee machine.
The cats are fed and water is replaced in their bowls. The
lion's share of the day is taken up with the grading of stu-
dent compositions. "Virginia," at her reproduction colonial Williamsburg desk in her bedroom on the second floor,
annotates a stack of process analysis essays with marginal
notes and end commentary, affixes a grade, and then
records it in an authentic roll book. This routine is sometimes interrupted by the writing of checks for the monthly
bills or the watching of daytime serials on an antiquated
pre-cable, pre-remote television. Occasionally, the tele-
phone rings with an unsolicited offer of the installation of
aluminum siding or replacement windows. Actual mail is
delivered by a uniformed federal employee each day the museum is open. As evening comes on, the boys play basketball on a court in the garage driveway while the girls play
house, taking turns emulating their mother by grading mock

papers at a desk in their playhouse. After watering the day-
lilies in the borders, "Virginia" calls out for pizza, which
will be delivered in less than half an hour, and passes the
time, after setting the table, by listening to a record of a
period band, "The Talking Heads," play on the stereo, re-
produced accurately from the obsolete analog technology
of vintage vinyl disc, stylus, and turntable.

Preserved Justice of the Peace Office
Metz

The front parlor of a two-story, four-square house, ordered
from the Montgomery Ward catalogue and delivered by
the Big Four Railroad in 1927, is the preserved office of
Metz's Justice of the Peace, Sander Vinkle. It has been restored to represent its condition circa early 1950s, when
Vinkle and other Justices of the Peace in villages along the
border with Michigan played a key role in providing
"quickie" marriages to out-of-state couples, since Indiana
had no waiting period or blood testing requirement. The
tableau of wax figures posed here is meant to recreate the
evening that Vinkle, in the period bathrobe, assisted and
witnessed by his wife, Velma, married Malcolm and Betty
X, of Detroit, in one such civil ceremony a half century
ago. Of special note is the room's authentic furniture and
decorations, all designed by Charles and Ray Eames, and
manufactured by the Herman Miller Company of Zeeland,
Michigan. Marriages are still performed on site every Tues-
day and Thursday from 1:30 until 4:15, though after-hour
nuptials can be arranged in an emergency. Pictures may be
taken with the mannequins. Rice may not be thrown, though
bird seed may be substituted as an acceptable alternative.
The driveway basketball court is lighted and open to the
public, who must provide their own balls and equipment.
There are no shower facilities on the site. The Metz Cham-
ber of Commerce, under whose auspices the house is
opened and maintained, assumes no responsibility for in-
jury, loss, or damage. You must enter at your own risk.

WARS, BATTLES,
SKIRMISHES, CIVIL UNREST

The Battle of Corydon
Corydon

Along with Gettysburg, the Battle of Corydon was one of only two Civil War conflicts fought on Northern soil. The battle at Corydon, once the state's capital, saw elements of Morgan's Raiders and a detachment of the 13th Alabama Light Infantry (Hornsby's Own) cross the Ohio River at Maukport in a predawn sortie designed to cripple the Union's ability to manufacture office furniture. The expected resistance of the Indiana Home Guard never materialized, as most of the regiment, sympathetic to the rebel cause to begin with, joined the invaders as they lay siege to the village. Blows were struck, finally, at the Christmas tree farm of Hiram Berry, when a battery of Rhode Island Zouaves (enroute to join Grant at Vicksburg), and the trumpet and flute sections of the Iron Brigade's mounted band (returning from a gig at the Turner's Club in Indianapolis) repelled the enemy in the salient known as The Bumble Bee's Hangover. Fought in the dark, the skirmish proved, ultimately, inconclusive. There were no human casualties, though three pigs and a goat were captured by the rebels and later barbecued by Confederate forces once back safely in Kentucky.

The 1879 Carbonate Riots and
The Wars of Alum Succession
Along the Corridor Stretching from Fort Wayne
and Terre Haute

Cylindrical markers in the shape of monumental baking soda tins in both these cites (important in the protracted history of this conflict) commemorate the dispute between forces seeking to introduce a new leavening agent standard to the baking public in the wake of the formation of the European Yeast Cartels. The Quick Bread Trail, as it is known, running between Fort Wayne and Terre Haute, includes the restored station of the underground railway in Carbon, the ruins of a government bauxite smelter in Roll, the annual Hoe Cake Festival in Danville, an hourly reenactment of the Massacre of the Innocents in Elwood (where two dozen duroc hogs were slaughtered by Pinkerton operatives in the aborted Lard Coup of Tipton County), the preserved Plains of Ossian with its assorted restored caissons and chuck wagons on display, and the larger than life Diorama of the Battle for Boxley. Butler University history Professor Emma Lou Thornborough's book, *The Uprising Uprising: The Indiana Wars of Alum Succession*, was awarded the Pulitzer Prize in 1952.

The First and Second Daylight Savings Wars
of 1948 and 1955
Various Locations North of US Highway 24

Hostilities broke out first at a Warsaw green grocery that summer between forces representing farmers and drive-in theater owners at odds over Indiana's adoption of Standard Time and its Daylight Savings variation. Largely a clandestine guerrilla action fought mostly at night and mainly by Mexican mercenaries against bands of volunteers recruited in Hollywood and known as the Victor Mature Brigades, the action focused in and around Stokely's canning plants and the outdoor cinemas of northern Indiana, but included also the highjacking of several soybean grain trains, the arson of a half dozen traditional movie houses, and the Great Popcorn Embargo which, oddly, devastated both sides. The conflict ultimately drew in the state's two military academies, Culver and Howe, after the showing of the Charlton Heston picture *The Private War of Major Benson* at the Wakarusa Drive-In resulted in a rumble that decimated the cadet classes of 1955. An uneasy peace was brokered by John Cameron Swayze that autumn with the signing of the Mishawaka Accords. This tense truce between the combatants, their ranks thinned through attrition and the introduction of new media which reduced market share, continues to this day.

The Tomb of the Unknown Chaplain
The Former Military Chaplain School
Fort Benjamin Harrison (Closed)
Marion County

Constructed at the end of The Great War, the modest limestone crypt on the site of what was once the Armed Forces Military Chaplain School at Fort Benjamin Harrison (now closed and transferred to the Unigov Planning Commission for civilian redevelopment) remains empty since all religious personnel serving in this nation's armed conflicts have been accounted for at the time of this writing. Access to the site is by means of the mowing crew during the spring and summer growing seasons.

Surplus Equipment Park
The American Legion Mall
Indianapolis

Stretching from the American Legion Headquarters, between Pennsylvania and Meridian Streets in downtown Indianapolis, is a grassy mall that has been, since the end of World War II, a vast military vehicle park, ordnance

dump, and staging motor pool for the disposition of surplus equipment to be used as memorials and monuments
at sites around the country. There are rows of 37mm antitank guns, howitzers of various calibers (all spiked, their
breech blocks gone), files of quad .50 mounts and Bofors
guns. There are hundreds of half-tracks and two-and-a-halfs,
jeeps, and even a few motorcycles with sidecars left over.
Tanks include a variety of Shermans, some Stuarts, and
even a Grant or two, destined for a park somewhere or
perhaps to be cemented in a town square or shopping mall.
The Legion faithfully distributes this surplus to its local
posts and to other interested veterans groups, to be set up
on the stoops and front lawns of the lodges and halls, next
to the lighted flagpoles, which are themselves made of
melted armour plating salvaged from the scrap of captured
Panzer tanks.

The Cleopatra's Barge Incident
The Ohio River

On June 9, 1997, the barge Cleopatra, a gambling river
float owned by the Caesar's Palace gaming concern and
moored at New Albany, strayed into the territorial waters
of Kentucky when it failed to execute a proper reversing
move near the Falls of the Ohio. The barge, displacing
1378 tons and generating almost a million dollars each
evening from its casino business, immediately came under
fire from shore batteries in Louisville and was boarded (after an engagement with three torpedo boats and a midget
submarine which fouled her rudder further, toppled her
radar mast, and severely damaged her ability to launch
and recover aircraft on her afterdecks) and towed to the
Kentucky shore (while being strafed by desperate helicopter gunships of the Indiana Wildlife and Fisheries Department) where her passengers and crew were ransomed after
three months of captivity in Louisville's Galt House Hotel.
The barge was later scuttled by a raiding party of Indiana
Marine Police, creating a hazard to navigation that the Army

Corp of Engineers then condemned and demolished further. What remains of her hulk, now used as an artificial reef off the patio of a riverside seafood restaurant, may be seen, with the aid of binoculars, from the Indiana shore.

The License Plate Insurrection and Bloodless Coup of Indiana's Secretary of State on 22 August, 1979
Statewide

In the summer of 1979, public outrage directed toward Ralph Otter, the then Secretary of State, boiled over into a bloodless coup d'etat which toppled his administration and precipitated a 72-hour imposition of marshal law, initiated by the governor as he hurriedly returned home after cutting short a trade mission to the Benelux countries. Animosity toward the Secretary had been growing throughout his tenure, a result of his unrestrained, capricious, and imperious exertion of power as well as his demonstrably bad prose style and poetic tin ear. Immediately upon ascending to office, Otter, a renderer and son of a defrocked accountant born in Michigan, ordered, as his first official act, the adoption of a new design for all the state's automotive tags which abandoned the traditional use of the state's universities' colors and deleted the state's motto, "The Hoosier State," replacing it with the highly offensive and objectionable "Heritage State." The revulsion to such a move was immediate and widespread. All of Indiana's newspapers editorialized against the change, the legislature met in special session as a committee of the whole and passed a resolution, the governor distanced himself, leaving on a fact-finding mission to the Greek island of Skyros, after appointing a blue-ribbon commission to report on the alternatives to prison manufactured metal plates. Soviets of local citizens were formed in most townships and cities. Ministers and priests sermonized from the pulpits. There were mass hunger strikes and bake sales called by many school districts. Road blocks were established by revolting

barracks of state troopers. Adams and Noble counties'
Offices of Motor Vehicles were vandalized, and stolen
records smeared with pig's blood. The agitation culminated
on August 22nd when a news conference hastily called by
the Secretary was disrupted by the poet Jared Carter (who
had arrived in Indianapolis earlier that day from Chicago
where he had fled upon the Secretary's inauguration, traveling in a sealed Pullman sleeper on Amtrak's train, *The
James Whitcomb Riley*, and supported by a cadre of uniformed
MFA students from Purdue and Indiana Universities), forc-
ing the Secretary to abdicate in the revolving restaurant at
the top of the downtown Hyatt Hotel. Since then the 4th
Monday of August is set aside as the Glorious Revolution of
August 22nd and celebrated in the state with parades of
automobiles, the ceremonial writing of haiku by elementary-
school children, the burning of Ralph Otter in effigy, and
the careful renaming of streets and buildings.

ART

The Musée de Bob Ross
Muncie

Housed in the converted and renovated Ball Brothers Department Store in downtown Muncie, The Musée de Bob Ross is home to the world's largest collection of works by the late master, Bob Ross. Over eight thousand paintings are in inventory, while several hundred are displayed at any one time in the museum's twelve galleries. The characteristic landscapes and seascapes (most of them painted live while being taped during his widely syndicated television show produced by Muncie Public TV) are displayed chronologically to give the visitor a sense of Ross's progression of technique and his many chromatic periods, which culminate in the final umber phase predominant at the time of his untimely death. With a palette more extensive than every major artist save Delacroix, Mr. Ross's repetitive rendering of his special motif, a placid lake in an ancient fir forest, is made new with each painting. The artist's actual palettes are, themselves, displayed on the mezzanine, where the visitor can appreciate Bob Ross's meticulous craft in the mixing of his paints, preserved in a kind of fossil record which, in its energy and élan, rivals the most enthusiastic abstract expressionist works. Also of interest is the faithful recreation of the artist's studio (in what was once women's lingerie) where Mr. Ross's easels, his primed and stretched canvases, and his tubes of paint are arrayed in the manner they were found upon his passing. Here too are the myriad variety of brushes and palette knives, as well as his extensive collection of combs and hair picks, and a selection of his favored models, such as a potted Norfolk Island Pine, a boulder from Jasper Beach, Maine, and a sky chart from the National Aeronautic and Space Administration showing the different categories of clouds. In the museum's entry vestibule, a bank of television monitors constantly features tapes of the master at work. Those tapes, along with poster, postcard, and refrigerator magnet reproductions of the work, may be purchased in the tastefully appointed gift shop, where the visitor will also discover the complete library of Mr. Ross's instructional media. There is also The Happy Little Tree Cafe, which specializes in nouvelle cuisine.

Cult of the Dead
Near Bedford

After an abortive attempt to construct a tourist destination theme park using an exact replica of the Great Pyramid of Cheops (made with limestone salvaged from the depressed local industry) as its main attraction, promoters declared bankruptcy in 1987 and allowed the grounds, which straddle old US 37, to fall into disrepair. Only recently have authorities noticed that the pyramid and its remaining buildings have been inhabited by a secretive—though by all accounts gentle—cult, modeling itself on the Egyptian Book of the Dead. Its members seem mainly to be recent graduates of nearby Indiana University who are unable to return to normal life after four years in Bloomington. It is said by many native inhabitants of nearby Bedford that the cultists are experimenting with mummification, buying cube ice, sunscreen, and batteries at Millard Weiss's Sunoco Station down the road for just that purpose. The local neighborhood crime watch reports many informants witnessing the incessant playing of Ultimate Frisbee and mass afternoon siestas on rope hammocks strung amongst the old steel derricks and cranes. It is a haunting and disturbing sight with partially clothed or even nakedly lethargic cultists draped over the massive blocks and worked stones strewn about the property, as others ritually bathe in the adjacent quarry whilst the humid Indiana twilight falls. Raids by the Monroe and Morgan County sheriffs' departments have failed to dislodge what appears to be the growing inhabitation, nor has the routine deployment of

modern psychological warfare (the continuous broadcast-
ing of amplified hard rock music) appeared to have had
any effect on the milling population. Their fires are seen
burning through the night. Rain crows make their lone-
some cooing cry. The cultists sleep in the shadow of the
gigantic pyramid. At the breached and rusted gate are the
abandoned hulks of their vehicles, mute testimonies of those
who believed, once, that they would be returning to civili-
zation, returning shortly to their families and friends with
some interesting stories to tell.

Our Lady of the Big Hair and Feet
Jasper

An evangelical order, founded in the 12th Arrondissement
of Paris during the reign of Louis Phillippe, established a
community in this country in the southern tier of New
York State in 1931. The nuns, refugees from the Second
Marcel Inquisition in Marseilles of the previous winter,
opened a convent in Indiana (a daughter of the mother
house in Elmira) two years later. Taking as their founding
instruction the gospel verses and associated apocrypha de-
scribing Mary Magdalene washing, with her hair, the feet
of Jesus, the sisters proselytize while coifing hair, doing fashion make-overs, and performing pedicures on the penitent.
One of the few cloistered orders given special papal dis-
pensation, in 1899, to actually touch the lay parishioners,
the sisters maintain The New Hoosier Beauty College and
Podiatry Clinic on the west side of the picturesque court-
house square. Hairstyling, shampooing, cutting, comb-outs,
corn-rowing, streaking, permanents, processing, and tint-
ing are all free. Appointments are accepted, but walk-ins
are cheerfully welcomed. The sisters, even after the Vatican
Councils, continue to don the habit of the religious and
are recognized by their flowered-print shifts with plastic
transparent aprons, open-toed white sandals, and patent
vinyl purses. Their wimples are made of bone barrettes

which secure teased, ratted, streaked, and volumized human and other species of natural hair and/or fur.

Perfection Biscuit
Fort Wayne

The Sunbeam Bakers of Perfection Biscuit, a nineteenth-century utopian community, led by the Silesian Prophet Basil Crandic, was established in Fort Wayne because of its ready access to rail lines and milled red winter wheat. After the Carbonate Riots of 1879, in which the village's secular residents destroyed the group's first bakery on Superior Street (a result of misplaced anxiety over anaerobic reproduction performed within), the bakers selected their current location on Main Street next to Allen County Ford. A Neo-Platonist apostasy, the bakers follow, in abject poverty and utter humility, a rigorous regimen in which they bake simple loaves of white bread. The bread, once baked, is never eaten nor sold, but each loaf is shellacked and stored secretly in warehouses all over the city in anticipation of an imminent rapture and the resulting reign of ideal forms, once the creation of the perfect loaf triggers the apocalypse. In order to support the order, the bakers manufacture prayers which are marketed in local gift shops, as well as the Indiana Home Grown concessions found at the state's major airport terminals. The prayers may also be purchased via the internet from the bakery's own web site commissary, www.perfection.org.

The Hoosier Herms
Throughout the State

These cairns, erected near rural crossroads throughout the state, are thought to be the work of pagan revivalists or the creators of the crop circle pictographs, who turned to the construction of stone columns once their counterfeit cereal creations were exposed (by the Discovery Channel in 1996) as not the work of aliens from space but of a couple of inebriated adolescents from Geneva who got the idea watching The Learning Channel in the late 80's. The Herms come in all sizes and shapes, and are made of many kinds of rocks, boulders, and pebbles. They all, however, share the unique characteristic of sporting a protruding stone phallus about half way up the shaft's length. This accouterment has, itself, sparked an additional religious movement (traced back to a group of iconoclastic Mormon Missionaries near Nashville) whose members, after seeing a special on House and Garden Television, began to scour the countryside searching for the offending structures. They then affixed a tent-like apparatus to the Hermes outcroppings, a symbol of the virtue of modesty and an illustrative demonstration of safe sexual practices. A year ago, Bill Moyers hosted a five-evening, twelve-hour PBS special on these phenomena, tapes of which are still available through your local affiliate during the twice yearly fundraising marathons.

Kosher Swine
The Holy City of Anderson

Rejecting the innovations in animal husbandry introduced by the colleges of agriculture at the nation's land grant institution, this sect of retrograde Ammonites practices traditional methods of hog rearing which eschew the modern penchant for complete confinement systems and industrial slaughtering, butchering, and curing. Hogs are allowed, if not encouraged, to roam unmolested through the town, to root in people's yards and fields, sample the various nut offerings left on doorsteps, and dispose of kitchen scraps and sacramental slop presented each day by selected field hands. The municipality maintains several wallows. Breeding is done naturally, since the sect refrains from castrating boars. Farrowing is also done on the ground and in the open without means of synthetic hormonal labor inducement treatment or the application of subtherapeutic pharmacology. Manure is regarded as an asset and not a liability, and it is liberally distributed on the streets of the town, which are strictly maintained as dirt or mud thoroughfares. Slaughtering, which is constantly performed beneath the nearest sturdy acorn-bearing tree, in order to hoist (by means of sanctioned and blessed block and tackle) and bleed the expertly stuck pig, is closely supervised by one or more members of the itinerant and coverall-clad clergy to assure quality and to exact the proper dietary standards from the procedure. It is said that there are more smokehouses in Anderson than human domiciles and that seems to be the case. The metal sheeting of hundreds of smokehouses, zoned and arrayed neatly in their own neighborhood, is often painted bright primary colors and creates an attractive backdrop to the snuffling surviving shoats as they forage between the buildings.

Movable Mountain
Off the Toll Road
Near Rolling Prairie

A hermit of the Archimedean Heresy has constructed this artificial mountain using discarded house jacks, porch screws, automobile racks and lifts, freight elevators, old fork lifts, cranes, derricks, water rams, and hydraulic pumps. The mountain, visible from the Indiana Toll Road, currently measures 728 feet above sea level, which is three feet taller than the highest natural point in the state (which may be found between Arba and Bethel near the Ohio border). The mountain continues to elevate at a rate of 2 inches a month. As its builder exhausts the vertical uplift potential of the lowest level's apparatus, he immediately undermines it and begins a new layer of machinery, encompassing an even broader base. The effect, from the vantage of the surrounding flat plain, is of a mountain of rusting metal crags and crevasses, cliffs of sheet steel and knobs of knurled rebar, girders and I-beams all trussed with turnbuckled wire cable and compressed springs, and illuminated at night by the occasional flood light, navigational strobe, or flashing safety beacon. The mass is at times punctuated by the exhalation and venting of steam or smoke, and reverberates with the twang of snapping wires as it settles and strains against the constant rising pressure from below. In the winter, acolytes and altar boys make artificial snow, launching it upon the mountain's flanks by means of blowers powered by small aircraft engines. The hermit, when not raising the mountain to new heights, lives on its summit in a simple hut where he will, at times, entertain visitors who seek an audience, though such meetings are, as reported by the pilgrims, somewhat disappointing. The hermit is often given to long periods of silent meditation or sleep. While most climb to the top, the peak is handicapped accessible by means of an electric vertical railway equipped with a rack and pinion cog prime mover. The view from the pinnacle, however, is said to be stunning. As one looks down on the vale below with its gently rolling river of cars and trucks, the thrumming harmonic of mutually suspended and compressed tension at play in the mountain's supporting architecture vibrates through one's entire body.

The Indians of Indiana
Whiting

The ashram is home to several hundred Indians who emigrated to the United States twenty years ago from the area around the region of Jodhpur. Enamored by depictions of American Indians gleaned from Indian television, the community sees, as its sacred calling, the recreation and preservation of Native American culture in its original setting. Its guru, the charismatic though reclusive Tecumseh Ramanathan, leads a pilgrimage every summer to the Tippecanoe battlefield for the Midwest's largest *powwow*. The congregation, moving south through the countryside by rivers and drainage ditches (by means of canoes and flat-bottom rafts), also utilize the ancient portage routes between continental watersheds. In 1992, the ashram achieved an international notoriety when the singer Pat Boone, actresses Mia Farrow and Shelly Long, architect Michael Graves, and several members of the Indiana Pacers basketball team briefly joined the group and were photographed by *People* magazine sitting with Ramanathan in the doorway of the communal sweat lodge. The ashram was subsequently rocked by scandal when simmering internal conflicts (stemming from disputes over the group's wealth and control of the international maize trade), coupled with rumors of fiscal impropriety and sexual misconduct, boiled over into the tabloids. Video clips showing Ramanathan reclining beneath a buffalo skin awning on the deck of a walnut travois, and being conveyed about the compound by a team of gray Percheron geldings became stock footage on the state's nightly news broadcasts.

AUTHOR'S NOTE

Michael Martone was born at St. Joseph's Hospital in Fort Wayne, Indiana, in 1955. It is interesting to note that the attending physician was a Doctor Frank Burns, Major, United States Army, retired, and recently returned to Fort Wayne following service in the police action in Korea. It was the same Dr. Burns, it turns out, who years later served as the model for the character "Frank Burns" appearing in the novel *M.A.S.H.* (authored by Richard Hooker) and in the movie and television versions based on the book. Martone recalls the modest premiere of the Altman film in 1970 and its initial screening at the Embassy Theater in downtown Fort Wayne. Dr. Burns, who had continued, after Martone's birth (it had been a difficult one, sunny side up, where forceps were used), to be his mother's gynecologist, arrived at the theater, the guest of honor, in a Cadillac Seville provided by Means Motor Company on Main Street. Sally Kellerman and Jo Ann Pflug also were there. All during the run of the television series, Dr. Burns, now in semi-retirement, happily appeared at strip-mall ribbon cuttings and restaurant openings, a kind of official goodwill ambassador, and took the ribbing from the public whose perception of his character had been derived from what they had read or seen in the movies and on television. His son, Frank, Jr., was two years ahead of Martone at North Side High School. Frank, Jr. anchored the 4x440 relay on the Redskin varsity track and field club where Martone served as team manager. Martone remembers Dr. Burns, team physician, coaching him in the use of analgesic balm and the scrubbing of cinders out from beneath the skin after a runner fell on the track. It was Dr. Burns who, later, diagnosed Martone's mother's ovarian cancer in 1979 and performed the failed hysterectomy that led to his mother's death that summer. It was Dr. Burns, still in his surgical scrubs, who met the family in the waiting room of St. Joseph's Hospital in Fort Wayne, the same hospital where Martone, twenty-four years before, had been born, delivered, by means of forceps, by Dr. Burns. The television was on, of course, an RCA model made in Bloomington, Indiana, and Martone remembers how hard it was not to watch it while, in a strange way, he also felt he was watching himself listening to Dr. Burns rehearse the final few minutes of his, Martone's, mother's life.